Prologue: The Girl   7

1. Approaching Danger   9
2. Secret Transformation   13
3. The Battle above the School   21
4. In the Bluescale Cave   29
5. Demonheart   35
6. Conversing with a Dragon   47
7. Facing the Council   55
8. Solving the Riddle   65
9. The Riddle's Answer   75
10. To Trust Again   85
11. Dragon Attack!   93
12. Flight Lessons   99
13. Iridigrarr   107
14. Bloodclaw Attack   113
15. Peace after the Fight   123
16. Demonheart's Torture   133
17. The Gemstone Warriors   141
18. A Hidden Helper   149

Acknowledgements   155
About the Author   157

THE POWER OF THE GEMSTONES

OF THE

GEMSTONES

REVEALING HER SECRET

by Izzyana Andersen

BOOK 1

in *The Power of the Gemstones* series

ISBN 13: 978-1-59298-594-4

Library of Congress Catalog Number: 2015920996

Printed in the United States of America

First Printing: 2016

20 19 18 17 16   5 4 3 2 1

Book design and typesetting by Dan Pitts

BEAVER'S POND
PRESS

Beaver's Pond Press
7108 Ohms Lane
Edina, MN 55439–2129
(952) 829-8818
www.BeaversPondPress.com

To order, visit www.ItascaBooks.com
or call (800)-901-3480. Reseller discounts available.

For more information, visit www.thepowerofthegemstones.com or follow The Power of the Gemstones on Facebook.

PROLOGUE: THE GIRL

In the world, there are heroes. Whether hidden or revealed, shy and bashful, queer and odd, or strong and brave, they all wait patiently for the time they shall rise . . .

Our hero looks like an ordinary thirteen-year-old girl. She may look ordinary, but she is not.

She has been hiding a secret. If society knew it, people would call her a monster, a beast, a freak of nature. And everyone would call her that, including you. She would be locked up in a laboratory for the rest of her life, the victim of ruthless experiments. Yes, this would all happen to her, so she keeps her secret locked away inside of her, away from all the prying human eyes of the world, even her friends'.

But secrets can never stay hidden for long; the truth is always revealed one day.

For Bella, that day is here.

CHAPTER 1

APPROACHING DANGER

Bella had an uneasy feeling.

What is wrong with me? she wondered. *Normally, I'm happy to be in school, especially if it's to work on math with my friends . . . but I feel like I need to run away.* Her stomach fluttered inside her like a wild bird trapped in a cage.

A voice interrupted her thoughts. "Hey, Bella, come on! We've got to get going!"

"Um . . . sorry, Paris." Bella sighed.

"What are you doing? Reading love notes?" Paris tried to peer into Bella's locker.

"NO! I have no interest in boys, and you know that!" She slammed her locker door shut. BANG! Paris jerked backward to avoid her nose being chopped off.

"Sheesh, watch out for people's noses," Paris grumbled, rubbing her nose and adjusting her glasses. "Let's get going! Raider and Gabby saved a table for us in the library! Come on!" And Paris zoomed off, her blonde hair waving behind her.

"Hey, wait up!" Bella called out, chasing after her friend. But the strange feeling did not leave her. *Why won't it go away?*

Bella entered the library and sat down with her friends. "Thanks for the sunny window spot."

"Bella, you're running late again!" Raider quipped.

"Oh? And how late am I this time?"

"One minute and two seconds!"

"Raider, just leave her alone," Gabby scolded. "Besides, she looks a little stressed."

"Well, you know the rule here at the Red Raven Middle School: you must always be on time!"

"Blah blah blah. Let's do some math!" Paris tap-tap-tapped her pencil on the table. Tap-tap-tap.

This annoyed Bella, but she became lost in worry. The ominous feeling grew stronger.

"Emer!"

Bella froze.

"Emer! Listen to me!"

"Stonehorn?" Bella telecommunicated back to him. "What's wrong?"

"Get out of the school!"

"Why?"

"There's danger coming! Run away! Now!"

With that, his voice left her mind. Bella glanced out the window.

She saw a red cloud approaching the school. Black wings were beating in it.

She leaped up in shock. Her chair crashed to the floor. Everyone in the library stared at her.

"Bella?" Raider asked.

"Daydreaming again," Paris reassured him.

"I must go. You have to leave, too," Bella warned, her voice shaking. "Everyone's in danger here."

"What's happening?" Raider asked. His green eyes were filled with worry.

She froze, uncertain what to say. *I must get out in order to save them.* With that thought, she ran out of the library.

As she dashed down the hallway, the attack began.

Lights flickered.

Fierce growls filled the hall.

The smell of smoke seeped into Bella's nose.

And the students' screams filled the air as the whole school panicked.

CHAPTER 2

SECRET TRANSFORMATION

Raider watched Bella run from the library.

"Bella! Wait!" he called out. *What's going on? Why is she upset?*

"We've got to go after her!" Gabby leaped up from her chair.

"Let's go!" Paris said.

THUD!

Raider turned around to find Gabby sprawled on the floor.

"I'm sorry! I tripped over a book!"

"Splendid," Paris grumbled.

"Let's just help her up and then find Bella," Raider said. Paris sighed, but Raider could tell she agreed with him. They ran back to Gabby, going the opposite way of the other panicked kids, who were pushing and shoving one another to get out.

"I'm sorry I held you two up," Gabby said. "You should have just run on without—" She burst into a coughing fit.

The smoke! It's getting harder to breathe, Raider realized. *And we're the only people left in here.*

Raider and Paris grabbed Gabby's hands and pulled her off the floor.

Gabby coughed as a growl filled the air. "What was that?!"

"I don't know. I don't like it. Let's get the heck out of here!" Paris shouted. They began running toward the door.

Before they could escape, however, part of the roof collapsed and blocked the door.

"We're TRAPPED!" Gabby cried.

"No, we're not!" Paris shouted. "We're going to climb out on this rubble. Follow me! And quit crying, Gabby."

But before they could do anything, something else blocked their way as it landed with a THUD.

No, Raider thought, *this is not possible.*

A beast stood before them. Its yellow catlike eyes scanned them. The three silver demon horns on its head glinted in the sunlight. Its sharp black talons grasped the rubble beneath it as its tail, covered in sharp silver spikes that ran along its back, lashed about. Its black wings towered overhead. Its bloodred scales and silver chest shone in the sunlight. It bared its awful teeth as smoke poured out of its nostrils.

The creature in front of them was a DRAGON.

Without thinking, Raider scrambled under a table.

"Oh, dear!" Gabby collapsed onto the floor in a faint.

The dragon clawed its way in her direction.

Gabby's in trouble! Raider thought. *I can drag her under the table to keep her safe!* Raider ran out from his hiding place and grabbed Gabby's limp arms.

A fearsome growl made him look up.

He stared into the yellow, soulless eyes of the worst thing he had ever seen in his life.

Terrified, he pulled Gabby to the table as the dragon advanced toward them.

"Hey, leave my friends alone!" Paris yelled. She grabbed a brick and threw it at the dragon's head. Raider was impressed.

WHACK! The dragon screeched.

"Don't worry, Raider, I'll fend off this overgrown lizard!" Paris shouted. She hurled another brick at it.

GLONK! The dragon, now raging with anger, lunged at Paris and snatched her up in its talons.

"PARIS!" Raider shouted from his stance in front of the table.

"Hey! Let me go!" She pounded her fists on the dragon's claws, but it simply ignored her as it took off through the hole in the roof.

Raider yanked Gabby under the table and tried to wake her up. "C'mon, Gabby, wake up," he muttered. *Paris was captured by the dragon, Gabby's out cold, and*

Bella is gone. Why did she run away? Why is all this chaos happening?

A roar filled the air as the returning dragon flipped the table over. Paris was not with the dragon.

"AAAGH!" Raider yelled.

The dragon flicked Raider away from Gabby.

Raider slammed into a bookshelf and fell to the ground. His whole body seethed with pain.

He watched with horror as the dragon clawed its way over to Gabby and plucked her up by the back of her shirt. She was still out cold.

Raider would not let this dragon take his friend. Though he was scared of the dragon and scared of getting hurt, he knew Gabby might die. Remembering Paris, he grabbed a brick and hurled it at the dragon.

BONK! The brick hit the dragon.

The dragon clawed its way over to Raider and snatched him up in its empty talon. Its warm, rough scales rubbed against him. Its claws smelled of smoke and blood. Raider looked at the beast. Its yellow eyes gleamed with terrible pleasure.

He stayed still. Glancing around, he saw that Gabby was in the dragon's other talon.

The dragon stumbled over to the hole in the roof and jumped up into the air. Raider's stomach lurched inside of him. He found himself above the school, surrounded by other red dragons like his captor. These dragons were burning the school.

Why are they doing this? he wondered. *They captured Paris, who might not be alive anymore, Gabby and me, and no one else? Instead, they're burning down the school? No more hostages? Hmm . . . maybe this is a capture-who-you-need-and-eliminate-witnesses mission.*

Suddenly, the talon released him, and he tumbled, along with Gabby, onto the metal floor of a cage. Paris was already there. SLAM. The dragon locked the door.

"Hey, let me out, you foul smoke-stench-fang-tooth-school-burning-cat-eye-silver-horned coward of a beast!" Paris yelled at the dragon flying around the outside of the cage. "And you! You there holding the cage in the air! You're all that I said, too!" She pounded the metal bars, her fists clashing against the metal with echoing clangs, her blue eyes flashing with fury.

"Paris! You're alive!" Raider said with relief.

"Of course I am!" she snapped. "Why wouldn't I be?"

"I thought the dragons would have . . ."

"Ugggh . . . where am I?" Gabby moaned, sitting up. Her glasses were bent and tilted, her hair was askew, and her olive eyes looked weakly around.

"We've been trapped in a cage by these demon-drag-ons above our burning school." Paris shook the bars of the cage, but to no avail. She slumped down on the ground, grumbling to herself.

"WHAT?!" Gabby sat straight up.

Paris and Raider nodded.

"What about Bella? Where is she? Did she get away?"

"I wish I knew," Raider mumbled to himself.

* * * * *

Crunch. Crunch. Crunch.

The dry grass beneath Bella's feet crackled and crunched as she looked for a place to hide. The dragons were attacking the school and lighting it on fire. She had seen kids evacuating the school, but she was worried about her friends.

I wish I had stayed there to help them. They don't know what's going on. Even I have no idea why they're attacking the school. Ugh, I just need to stop worrying and get back to them as soon as I'm done . . .

"Emer!"

"Yes, Stonehorn?" she telecommunicated back to him.

"I thought I would inform you that reinforcements are on the way. We can hold back the attack and send them crawling back to their crummy dirt home."

"That's a relief." An abandoned bus barn caught her eye. She dashed into it, making sure no one was around.

"Do you think you'd be up to helping us fight? If you don't want to, I understand. After the last battle you were in—"

"I'm fine, Stonehorn." She cut him off, a sting in her voice. "I'll help. I'm in the mood for fighting some pests, anyway."

"Just find Knifeclaw in the air, and he'll tell you what to do. I wish you luck!"

"Thanks." His voice left her. Bella felt truly alone for the first time that day. The air felt stale around her. She could not focus on that, however. She had to concentrate on something much more important.

Okay, let's do this, she thought confidently. She placed her right hand over her heart. Bright light filled the bus barn.

And Bella began to change.

She grew shiny blue scales and a long, sleek tail with little green gemstones on its tip. Yellow-gold claws appeared on her now-blue hands as yellow-gold wings sprouted out of her back next to the spikes running from her head to her tail. Her hair turned into gold ram-like horns, curving along the back of her head. Her clothing morphed into her scales. Gold chest plates ran from her neck under her chest to the beginning of her tail, and a large green emerald flashed onto her chest.

Bella was no longer a human.

She was Emer, a dragon.

She grinned. "Now, I am ready."

CHAPTER 3

THE BATTLE
ABOVE THE SCHOOL

Emer smashed through the abandoned bus barn. Shards of wood flew everywhere as the barn collapsed into a tremendous heap. With her strong wings, she lifted into the air. As she gained altitude, she noticed blue dragons like herself flying above her. Their armor glinted in the sunlight as they began to attack the red dragons. All the battling beasts tumbled about in the air, blood dripping to the ground below.

"Excuse me, coming through," Emer said as she whipped her tail out, smacking two red dragons' heads. She stretched out her wings and grabbed the head of a red dragon on each wing talon, promptly flapping her wings downward to crack the two evil dragons' heads together. She flipped herself forward, slicing a black wing nearby with one of her claws and then barrel-rolling through a fight.

Spreading her wings, she rose higher and came face-to-face with an armor-covered dragon. This imposing creature was Knifeclaw, the battle general.

"Ah, so you made it, Emer," Knifeclaw thought to her.

"Yes, I'm here." She smiled. "Do you think we can talk instead of telecommunicating?"

"Emer, it's too risky here. There have been humans sighted in the area."

"Yeah, but they all evacuated a long time ago." Emer was confused.

"One of our warriors stated that he saw three humans being taken by the Bloodclaws. In fact, they're over there now." He pointed at a dragon flying away with a cage.

Emer squinted at the cage. *Something about those kids seems familiar,* she thought. As she looked closer, she gasped. *MY FRIENDS!* Without warning, she flew away from Knifeclaw after the red dragon.

"Emer! EMER! I DEMAND you come back here! NOW!" His voice roared so loudly in Emer's head that it hurt. But she ignored him and chased after the dragon carrying her friends.

She let her wings lift her up into a dive formation, falling downward just long enough to swoop at the Bloodclaw. Startled, it let out a screech.

You devil, she thought. *Your kind has ruined my colony's life, and now you want to take my friends. You deserve to die.* The Bloodclaw hissed, almost as if it had heard her thoughts.

Hiss at this! the voice in her head shouted. She grabbed one of the Bloodclaw's wings with her talons and raked her other claw down it. The dragon screeched in pain. Blood droplets fell from the shredded wing into the cage below.

"Aaaagh! It's raining blood!" Gabby screamed.

"And I won't be singing hallelujah to that!" Paris yelled.

They're safe. A glimmer of happiness sparked in Emer's heart. The Bloodclaw roared, and its tail smacked Emer's lower leg.

You're still dying. Emer hissed and sliced the dragon's face. Its shriek of pain hurt her ears. The pain must have startled it, because it dropped the cage.

Diving downward, she caught the cage as screams chorused from it. *Sorry, guys!* she thought.

When she faced the Bloodclaw again, it looked even angrier than before. It hissed and then began to charge at her.

You won't be going back to your leader to beg to do more harm. She held up her right claw; its scales began to change to an emerald green. *Sorry, not sorry,* she thought, just as it was in range. She lashed her claw right at its chest. Her claw plunged in with ease, and she shuddered as she felt the tissue around it shredding to pieces.

Giving one final cry, the Bloodclaw's wings ceased to beat, and it plummeted out of sight.

Emer felt something wet on her scales. Blood dripped down her forearms and chest. *Ick, I'm going to need a bath.* She snorted in disgust. *But at least I saved my friends.* She smiled, eavesdropping on their conversation.

"Oh, my . . ." Gabby whimpered.

"Holy cow, that was AWESOME!" Paris exclaimed. "She was like, 'Oh, you're gonna die,' and the evil dragon was like, 'Save me, oh, someone save me!' and she was like, 'BAM! SCRATCH! PUMMEL! SLAM!' and he fell to the ground like a weak little wimp!"

Raider laughed. "Yeah, those were some pretty amazing fighting skills."

Aw, thanks. Emer grinned as if her friends were actually telling her in person.

"EMER!" She looked up. Knifeclaw had flown over beside her, glaring down at her. "Why in the name of the Greatwing did you run away?" he telecommunicated.

"To help my friends! You would save your friends if they were in danger, too!"

"Yes, but my friends aren't humans," he spat. Emer's heart hurt at this, but she stayed strong.

"You've always said that we Bluescales need to protect every living creature from the Bloodclaws; this includes humans! So please help me find a place to hide them for now! Please!"

Knifeclaw's scarred eye stared at the ground in thought. Sighing, he finally replied, "Fine. I'll help. Just hand the cage to me, and I'll hide them somewhere they'll stay safe."

A smile spread across Emer's face. "Thanks."

Emer prepared to hand the cage over to Knifeclaw. However, fate had different plans. An awful roar pierced their ears as a Bloodclaw with a cracked horn and scarred eye flew up out of nowhere. Knifeclaw hissed in shock.

"Emer, move aside! Quickly!" Knifeclaw threw himself toward the evil dragon, talons outstretched, teeth prepared to bite, fire ready to incinerate the beast in front of him.

But this Bloodclaw was smarter than he looked. Slicing his black wings through the air, he flipped backward and lunged himself forward, his head ramming into Knifeclaw's underbelly, the one unarmored part on Knifeclaw's body.

"Argh!" Crumpling like a swatted fly, the Bluescale army commander sank a few feet in the air, but he regained his flight.

The Bloodclaw sped forward to attack Emer. She, however, was prepared. *Come and try to attack me, you red-scaled devilish coward!* With that, she lashed out her gem-encrusted tail at his eyes and slashed his underbelly with her sharp golden claws. That only enraged him, and he lunged forward, his right talon outstretched. It tore along one of her wing membranes. Pain and shock filled her body as she dropped in altitude. Blood droplets fell from the long cut as she tried to regain strength. It did not help that her friends were panicking below her.

"What are they doing?!" she heard Paris yell.

"They're fighting over us!" Raider explained.

"Well, who's going to win?"

"I hope the blue dragons do! They at least look sophisticated enough to wear armor to battle, and their eyes aren't that scary yellow!"

"And they're blue." Paris huffed a sarcastic sigh, and Emer could only imagine what cross-armed pose she was in right now.

"It doesn't matter that those blue dragons just happen to have the same hues as my favorite color! All that matters is that we live!"

CLUNK. "Great, Gabby fainted again!"

Again? Emer thought. *She fainted before this?*

"Stop focusing on those humans!" Knifeclaw's thought interrupted her eavesdropping. "Concentrate on—"

Everything was interrupted by a searing pain in her toes. The Bloodclaw, this peculiar, thorn-in-the-side Bloodclaw, had made a bloody cut along all her back talons holding the cage in safety. *I will not let go. I will not let go. I will not let go . . .*

The vicious dragon lunged out and smashed Emer in the gut with a full-out back talon kick. Emer flew backward from the force of the attack and the pain.

And the cage slipped free from her grasp.

"NO!" she yelled out loud, the cage falling directly into the Bloodclaw's back talons. He sliced his wings through the air and escaped from the battle, yelling out something in his strange, warped language that beckoned all his cronies to follow him back to their lair.

NO! Not my friends! Not Raider! Not Paris! Not Gabby! NO! Come back here, you foul no-good-evil-smoke-inhaling, yellow-eyed demon . . . ouch, she wheezed in exhaustion, her body complaining that it was too tired and injured to carry on this mission.

"Emer! Come back here to me! I'll get you home safely!" Knifeclaw called to her mind.

"But my friends—"

"Your friends will be fine! Remember, I will always care for your safety over any of the other dragons' safety! Your uniqueness makes you quite valuable. As for your human friends, well, humans are a stone a dozen; there are always more. Dragons, not so much. Come along now. Vladmir will fix you up."

"Knifeclaw—"

"This is an order!"

Emer glanced back. Her heart was torn. Past memories cut through her fragile mind. Every aching and bloody scale on her body wanted to go and save her friends from danger.

But she had no choice. She was too injured and battle-sore to continue to chase after her friends. And she would never hear the end of it from Knifeclaw about "You were given your dragon form for a reason—to interact with our superior species" and "Stop worrying about the humans. They're worth nothing but trouble."

But my friends aren't trouble, Emer thought to herself, her heart aching. *They're special, each one in his or her own way. Gabby can make anyone laugh at any time yet always knows when to get work done; Paris is so self-confident in the funniest way, and her sass always makes me smile; Raider . . . Raider is kind, smart, fun to be around . . . he's . . . well . . .* She sighed, thoughts swarming through her mind like a hive of buzzing bees. There were many of them, and they all stung in some way.

I'll find a way to save them, she concluded, *once I'm better. Why can't humans and dragons just get along? Why do I have to be stuck in the middle? Why do I have to deal with dragon pride, selfish humans, and evil dragons?*

Why am I the only Dralerian?

CHAPTER 4

IN THE BLUESCALE CAVE

"Ouch!"

"Calm down, Emer; this will be done in a minute," a steady voice comforted her.

"Rrrgh. Vladmir, I'm sorry for being so fidgety. It's just that this is my first wing tear, so—"

"It will hurt." He finished the sentence for her as he wove the needle through the torn membrane. "Every dragon's first torn membrane hurts, but it is a sign that you are brave."

"Bravery shmavery, my broken toe talon." She puffed a narrow plume of green fire from her mouth at the floor, grimacing as smoke began to billow out of her nose.

"I take it someone's mission did not go well." Vladmir sighed, knotting the end of the stitch with his old yet very nimble dragon fingers. As he stood to his full height and stretched, the light from the GlowCrystals on the wall reflected off his diamond-white scales.

"It's just that a bunch of Bloodclaws attacked the human school I go to and took my three friends." She watched smoke rise from her nose. "I tried to keep them safe, but dragons, of course, have to care about themselves more than about humans."

"Now, who says that?" Vladmir asked. She knew that she couldn't hide anything from him. He was the Bluescale wise dragon, the oldest and most knowledgeable of the dragons.

"Pretty much everyone above my rank. Knifeclaw says it; the Bluescales who despise humans say it; Majesty sometimes even says it." Green fire whished out of her mouth again, this time from exhaustion and annoyance.

"Just because you're half-human and half-dragon does not mean that you have to only take full pride in your dragon side." He reached up and took a jar of herbal salve and began to rub it on her bloody, swollen toes. "Look at me: I have white scales, wisdom, and more knowledge about the secrets of the ages. But am I arrogant about it?"

"No, but you can't transform from human to dragon as I can." She stared at the ground. "I wish Iridigrarr were here. Then I wouldn't feel so alone."

Vladmir stopped tending to her wounds. He gazed at her, staring right into her eyes. Bella felt as if she could see every ounce of knowledge and concern in his eyes, as well as the slight bags of age underneath them. "Now I see why you're so upset. The same events happened with Iridigrarr."

Emer nodded.

"Well, Emer," he said, deep in thought for a while as he bandaged her toes, "I see why you want to save your human friends. It just depends on what you truly care about. If it's your tribe and yourself, then you'll probably stay here. I know that you'll heal, but your friends might be lost forever. Then again, you could go save your friends from the grasp of evil, but you might hurt the wounds you have now or create new gashes or even die. Some tribe members might despise you for saving the humans. But it's up to you."

"Okay, well, thanks, Vladmir. Thanks for understanding." Emer stood up, wiggling her bandaged toes, wincing slightly in pain.

"You're welcome, Emer." His smile radiated with kindness and goodness, one that Emer liked when she was down.

As she pit-patted away from his room, she was lost in her thoughts. Half of her wanted to save her friends, but another half wanted to stay safe from harm and remain loyal to her tribe.

Suddenly, she overheard some voices.

"Well, what do we do?"

"Should we stay loyal to the dragon lineage or save the humans that the Bloodclaws took?"

Hm? What's going on? Emer glanced up. *And where am I? I've never been in this hallway before.* Looking around and listening, she found a small crack in the wall. As she listened to the voices, she gasped. *The meeting cave! I had no idea there was a crack here! And this is an exclusive meeting! What are they talking about?* Emer listened carefully.

"We should let them rot! Humans are the worst mistake the Greatwing made!" an angry Bluescale roared with the ferocity of a lion.

"Oh, be quiet, Battlescar," a feminine voice shushed him. "Some humans are good. Just because some killed off your family does not mean that they are all bad."

"Glitterscale, really?" Another voice intruded. "Humans—nice? I don't think so."

"Some humans are nice. Especially young ones. And those three humans they captured looked quite young."

"SILENCE!" a noble voice thundered. "We need more information. I've heard too many different versions of what really happened to decide on what to do."

"I know that only three were captured! That could mean something!"

"Like what?" someone scoffed.

"They could be from The Foretelling!"

"That's impossible! The Foretelling was only made as a bedtime story for draclings to reassure them the Bloodclaws will disappear! And they never will!"

"Then explain how Emer exists. She's an emerald Dralerian, and they're all supposed to be extinct."

And they're discussing me, once again. Emer huffed. *Why do they have to continually talk about other random topics instead of what's really important? Why can't there just be a dragon that decides to step up?* Suddenly, she felt a fiery sensation travel through her bones. She felt as if she could defeat anything that came her way.

"You know what?" she whispered to herself. "I will step up. I care about my friends. I have loyalty to them. Whether I die or not while trying to save them doesn't matter. A true warrior saves those in need, no matter what." And with those brave words, she found her way to the Flight Ledge and soared into the air, determined to rescue the prisoners.

CHAPTER 5

DEMONHEART

If there was any wise guy out there who wanted to complain about his terrible day, Raider wanted to tell him to quit complaining. No one on earth could be having the terrible day he was experiencing.

For one, he was in a cage—a cage being pulled by two red dragons into a dark tunnel. The cage jerked up and down as it slid down the rocky hallway. The newly attached wheels made it wobbly. The dragons that were pulling the children seemed to be growling to each other in a strange way, almost as if they were talking to one another.

"OH MY GOSH, I'M SO SCARED!" Gabby exclaimed. "They're going to kill us all! And gnaw on our bones! And chew on our skulls! And eat our organs and then I won't get to be a veterinarian, and my life will be ruined and—"

SLAP!

"OW!" Gabby yelled at Paris. "Why did you do that?"

"Look at you!" Paris scolded. "You're acting like a coward! You need to stop this!"

Gabby's eyes drifted to the ground. "I'm sorry," she said, "for acting this way. I'm just really scared."

"Gabby, all of us are," Raider reassured her.

"I'm okay," Gabby whimpered. She turned away, looking out from the bars.

"Good thing Gabby straightened up, or else I would have lost it," Paris muttered, leaning against one of the bars next to Raider. "What I'd like to know is, where is Bella?"

"Yeah, she just ran off, not even saying good-bye," Raider said. "You'd think she would stick around to help us out."

Why did Bella run off? he wondered, puzzled. *If there were any danger, she would protect us. It's just so strange . . . it's almost as if she knew it would happen.*

Thoughts flashed through his mind: Bella glancing out the window, a concerned look on her face full of worry, pain, and fear; Bella telling her friends to escape, to run away, and then running off herself . . .

She did know, he realized. *She knew the dragons were coming to attack the school. But how?*

His thoughts, however, were interrupted as a loud creaking noise coming from a concealed wooden door in front of them echoed off the stone walls and bounced all over.

"A door?" Gabby asked, looking confused. "Dragons use doors?"

"I guess." Paris shrugged.

"Wow, these creatures are intelligent enough to use doors." Raider eyed the door with both awe and panic.

The two dragons pulled the cage forward, the wheels squeaking louder than a thousand mice begging for cheese. As the cage creaked on, the friends saw an amazing sight: a vast open cavern. Its brown stony ceilings reached up to a near-impossible height, with fang-like stalactites protruding from it. Torches filled the room with an eerie, reddish glow.

"What—how—this—this isn't possible! How—why?"

"Raider, don't you start losing it now," Paris threatened with panic in her voice as her eyes dashed from here to there.

She's scared too; she just doesn't like to show it, Raider realized. *Even though she believes in dragons, I don't think she expected this.* He glanced over at Gabby's panic-stricken face, and he knew she was scared out of her wits.

"ARGREE NAR ARR GROWK!" one of the Bloodclaws exclaimed to its partner.

"EYIARR!" the second one shrieked, dashing out of the room, claws click-clacking down the hallway.

"WER NA ME!" the first one called out, almost trampling the other as it scurried from the room.

It sounds like they were scared of something and running away in a panic, Raider worried. "Hey, Paris, Gabby, do you think we should be worried about what they just did?"

"I-I don't know," Paris stuttered. "Gabby? What do you think?"

Gabby did not respond.

"Gabby?" both Raider and Paris asked. She was standing in a corner of the cage, as petrified as the stones around them.

"Look," she whispered. "Look."

What they saw terrified all of them.

A large red dragon sat on an ornately chiseled stone throne. It looked exactly like the dragons that had attacked their school, only it was twice the size of the others and had black markings over its eyes, which glinted with evil. His sharp claws were made to attack. His pointed teeth were ready to kill.

This was a monster.

"Who are you?" Raider demanded, summoning up all his courage.

"Oh!" the monster's eyes lit up as he saw the children. "What do we have here?"

"I don't know. Three children who'd like their lives to go back to normal?" Paris asked.

The monster barked out a laugh, the kind that stung Raider's ears. "You weaklings certainly are quite the entertainment, aren't you?"

"Listen! We have no idea who you are!" Raider said. "You probably mistook us for someone else. So just let us go."

"PLEASE!" Gabby cried.

"Ah, the human children beg for freedom," the monster mused, glancing at his claws. "But, alas, there shall be none."

"Why?"

"Well, that reason has a long history behind it, which you groundlings do not need to worry about. All you need to know is that you might be the ones from The Foretelling."

Raider's eyes shot open. "The Foretelling?"

"The Foretelling . . . I don't like the sound of that." Gabby glared at the dragon, suspicion in her eyes.

"The Foretelling?" Paris asked, astounded. "AWESOME!"

"You might be, or you might not be. I don't know," the dragon growled. "However, my head assistant here, Scareye, will check." A smaller red dragon slithered up from nowhere. Scars covered his scales, tears were scattered over his wings, and his center horn was cracked. But the scar over his right eye, white and blind, was what made him as scary as the monster dragon.

His bloodstained claws made a peculiar click-click as he walked toward them, like a person impatiently tapping his fingers. The children backed into a corner of the cage as Scareye's yellow eye scanned them.

"Hmmm . . ." he pondered, his voice dripping like oil. "One blue sapphire, one yellow sapphire, one ruby . . ."

"What!" the monster dragon shouted.

"Yes, Demonheart, these human hatchlings have the same gemstones as in The Foretelling."

Demonheart! Terrified shivers ran down Raider's spine.

"But do they have the Dragon Spirit? That's what would make them part of it."

"You know I have no expertise in that matter!" Scareye cried out.

"Well, find out! NOW! Or your head will be hung out for the crows to peck!"

Scareye nodded and glared at the humans, muttering curses under his breath.

Crack.

Raider looked around.

Crack.

Paris poked him with her elbow.

"Ow! What was that for?" he whispered.

"Shhh!" She pointed up. Raider did his best to look up at where she was pointing. At first, he didn't see anything, but a slight movement caught his eye. Whatever was moving up there was near a stalactite, and it seemed as if it was hitting it.

"Scareye, what is that infernal cracking noise?" Demonheart growled at his assistant.

"I have no idea. It's probably nothing. This is an old creaky cave."

As Raider watched, the mighty triangular rock gave a CRACK and fell to the ground. SMASH! The sharp rock piece drilled into the stone floor beneath it.

"What in the name of the Greatwing!" Scareye gasped, fear in his eyes as he jumped.

"It is I!" a blue dragon landing on the fallen stalactite cried out.

"It's you! You saved us earlier today!" Paris exclaimed, bursting with excitement and then pausing. "I don't know your name."

"Emer, the dragon warrior," Demonheart snarled.

"Yep, I'm here in all my dragony glory. Now let the humans go," she demanded.

Demonheart uttered a strange chuckle that covered Raider with chills. "Scareye, go show her what happens when other dragons, especially Bluescales, try to ruin my fun." An evil smile appeared on Demonheart's face.

Scareye snickered and began to run forward, leaping into the air. His mouth was open, and his teeth were sharp and dangerous looking.

BONK! Emer whacked her fist on his head. Scareye tumbled senseless to the ground.

"SCAREYE! Get UP! Get UP, you slime bag of an imbecile!" Demonheart yelled.

Emer did not seem affected. She appeared in front of the friends. Her claws flashed an emerald green, and she sliced through the metal bars of the cage.

"Whoa, how did you do that?" Paris exclaimed, a huge smile on her face.

"No time to explain now!" Emer said. "Hop on my back! Grab my scales and spikes and hold on!"

They did as she said. Her scales were warm. A blood-and-smoke smell lingered on her, but it was not strong. It felt as if there were something familiar about her.

"GET UP!" Demonheart screamed, his voice crackling as orange fire flew out of his mouth. Scareye did sit up and, seeing the situation around him, leaped off the ground and flew to the top of the cave. Fire and smoke steamed behind him.

"Can we leave now?" Gabby begged.

Their dragon warrior did not say a thing. She sat still for a while and then lunged forward, grabbing the cage in which they had once been captives.

Scareye dived down from the tall heights to which he had flown. He was almost close enough to hurt them.

CLANK! "Skueeeee!" Scareye wheezed, and smoke poofed out of his mouth as Emer rammed the edge of the cage into his underbelly.

"Scareye, instead of attacking me, why don't you go and blitz your pain of a ruler?" Emer pushed the cage forward, with the stunned Scareye still lying on its top.

"Scareye! SCAREYE! SNAP TO ATTENTION!" Demonheart shouted.

Scareye and the cage rolled straight toward his leader.

SMASH! CLATTER! BANG! Noises crashed in everyone's ears.

"Good," Emer muttered, and then she ran, her friends clinging desperately to her. She smashed through the wooden door, splinters flying everywhere.

"Your ram-like horns helped you smash through that door!" Raider exclaimed.

"I don't have time for science right now, Rai . . . I mean, strange kid I don't know."

"Have you ever rammed anyone's stomach?" Paris asked in jubilee.

Emer laughed. "Yes, I have occasionally. My claws are much more useful." She became serious. "Okay, you three humans are going to have to hold on even tighter now," she warned. "I'm going to dash between two Bloodclaws ahead so I can get you to safety. Got it?"

"Got it," Gabby and Raider said, both grasping desperately onto her shiny scales.

"I really got it. I do NOT want to die!" Paris said.

Emer charged forward. Two Bloodclaws stood ahead next to a narrow tunnel. As they saw her, they screeched with displeasure.

"Excuse me, I am leaving!" Green fire blasted out of her mouth, obliterating the Bloodclaws in front of her. They fell to the ground, charred and black as coal. She charged up the tunnel, cracked her way through the small door, and flew up into the open sky.

"Don't worry. The worst is over. Now you can relax." She tilted her head at them and smiled.

Raider was confused. *This dragon has come back for us again when we were in danger. She's smiling at us as if we are her own friends; she's done almost everything to save us. And her eyes . . . there's just a look in her eyes that reminds me of someone . . .*

A thought flashed through his mind. It was from the beginning of the school year, when a terrible bully had been hurting Paris and Gabby.

"Leave us alone!" Gabby had cried, tears dripping out of her eyes.

"Yeah, you awful pile of parasite-ridden bird dung!" Paris had hollered at the bully. His hand had squeezed her shoulder hard, and Paris had crumpled to the ground, whimpering in pain.

Raider had stood watching, too scared to do anything. That's when he had noticed Bella. She had finished talking with a teacher and had noticed the scene before her. He had seen a fire light her eyes. It had almost looked as if smoke was rising from her nose.

Bella had run and lunged at the bully, knocking him to the ground. She had pounded his face with her fists. He had managed to push her off and stand up again. She had leaped right back at him, striking his chin at a perfect angle. As he had tried to run away, she had kicked him in the gut and punched him in the nose. He had fallen to the ground, blood running from his nose.

The giant had fallen.

Gabby and Paris had been dumbfounded at what had happened. Raider had been both confused and impressed.

"Just remember," Bella had said, a strange seriousness in her voice, "if you ever need me, I will always help you, never expecting a reward. Wherever I am, wherever you are, and whatever is happening, I will come to your aid. I am always with you, even if you cannot see it with your eyes."

"What do you mean, 'not see it with my eyes'?" Gabby had asked.

"Yeah, that doesn't make any sense." Paris had stared at Bella.

Bella had smiled at that. "You'll see me with your heart. I know it."

Raider almost fell off Emer. He put Bella's words together.

"I am always with you, even if you cannot see it with your eyes."

"You'll see me with your heart."

"I know it."

Oh, my gosh. Raider was in shock. *It all makes sense. The smile, the eyes, the violent maneuvers, the way she has come to save us . . . it all connects. It's not scientific, but it makes sense. What if this dragon, Emer, is our friend Bella?*

CHAPTER 6

CONVERSING WITH A DRAGON

The flight back to the Bluescale cave was relaxing. The afternoon sun shone upon Emer, warming her light-blue scales. The spring air blew in her face.

"So, Emer, how exactly did you chop down that stalactite again?" Paris asked.

"I have a special ability that makes my claws extra sharp."

"Really? Do all dragons have that ability?" Gabby asked.

"Or breathe awesome green fire that obliterates everything around them?" Paris exclaimed.

Emer laughed. "No, only I have the sharp emerald claws and the green fire, though other dragons like me can breathe yellow-orange fire."

"Do they have emeralds on their chests? Like you?"

Emer found herself a little nervous at that question. "Um, no. I'm the only dragon that exists with an emerald."

"Oh."

"Hey, Emer, you know how you said we'd be going somewhere safe?" Gabby asked.

"Yeah."

"Where are we going? We were over a big forest area and then passed over prairie, and now we're over mountains! I have no idea where I am!"

"We're going to the Bluescale cave. It's hidden away in the Badlands of South Dakota."

"How do you know that those mountains are called the Badlands? And the name of the state?" Raider asked, suspicion in his voice.

Emer gulped. "I just learned it in Bluescale school."

"Who are the Bluescales?" Gabby asked.

"We're a tribe of dragons that defend all animals that the Bloodclaws threaten to kill. We live together in a colony that is just like a human city."

"How many dragons live in the cave?" Paris asked.

"I'm not sure. Somewhere between seven hundred and nine hundred."

"WOW!" all three kids exclaimed.

Emer could only grin at this. "Each dragon has his or her own special job," she said. "Almost all of us are fighters. But, when we're not fighting, we work as hunters or gatherers or teachers or blacksmiths or whatever. There's even a small group of us that stay in the cave year round and care for the other Bluescales."

"What do YOU do?" Paris asked; she was so excited that Emer thought she might fall off her back.

"I'm a warrior."

"What do you do in the meantime?" Raider asked.

"You're certainly nosy about my personal life," Emer growled at him.

"I was just curious," he replied, pretending to sound innocent. "After all, I have a friend who acts almost just like you."

Emer's heart began to beat fast. *What does he mean by saying that?* she wondered, her stomach joining her heart by doing flips. *Has he figured out that I, Emer, am also the human named Bella? And if he has, how does he know? Is he really that smart?*

She regained her composure to ask, "Who is this friend?"

"Oh, that's Bella he's talking about," Paris said.

"Or at least we thought she was our friend," Gabby said, sadness in her voice.

"She ran off before this happened."

"She never even said good-bye."

"Bella swore that she'd always protect us and always be with us."

"But what she did earlier today proved wrong."

Emer's heart saddened. Her friends thought she had betrayed them!

"You know, she might have just had to go do something." Emer did her best to answer casually, but she could not hide the shakiness in her voice.

"She ran off for nothing," Paris grumbled. "And look at what she missed."

"Bella always daydreams about mythical creatures," Gabby said. "She draws them, talks about them, reads about them, does math problems about them . . . who else does that?! And then when dragons actually turn up, she's nowhere!"

"Well, maybe she saw the Bloodclaws." The words fell out of Emer's mouth faster than she could stop them. *Oops.*

"The what?" her friends asked again.

"The Bloodclaws, evil red dragons with no living souls." Emer found herself growling at their very name. "They like to torture their victims, letting them die a painful death. Their leader, Demonheart, is the worst of all. Some dragons say that he's the devil put on this earth to torture all human- and dragonkind." By now, smoke was streaming out of her nose so thickly it was hard for her to see.

"Demonheart . . . that's the dragon that wanted to know if we were part of The Foretelling! Whatever that is!" Paris exclaimed.

"And the Bloodclaws! I bet Bella saw them approach the school and ran off in terror!" Raider said.

"But why would she run off? She probably didn't even know what they were. Did she?" Paris wondered aloud.

"I'd run if I saw them coming after me!" Gabby exclaimed. "Look!" All four of them looked backward. Three Bloodclaws were flying after them, smoke flowing from their nostrils.

"Oh, snake fangs," Emer growled. She thought she had escaped from them! *Demonheart probably sent them after me,* she thought. *Why in the name of the Greatwing is he so intent on capturing my friends?*

"Okay, you three need to hold on even tighter than before," she advised. "I'll have to perform evasive maneuvers in order to get rid of those Bloodclaws."

"Evasive maneuvers?" Gabby asked.

"Gabby, just calm down," Raider reassured her. "Everything will be fine."

"Yeah!" Paris yelled. "Keep calm and HOLD ON FOR YOUR LIFE!"

The three friends grasped tighter than ever onto Emer's scales. It hurt so much, she wondered if some of her scales might be pulled out. *I have no time to focus on that!* she scolded herself. *Right now, I've got to teach the Bloodclaws a lesson!*

Emer folded her wings and dived down between the rocky formations. She swooped nimbly between the stones around her.

CLUNK! A Bloodclaw smashed into a rock behind her.

Good. One down and two to go! Flapping her wings, she flew forward, her wings barely touching the mountains beside her.

The Bloodclaws were gaining.

Emer swooped through a hole in a rock and then swerved down. She was so low she could have touched the rocky ground beneath her. She heard the Bloodclaw closest to her snicker and then dive down.

Just as he almost had her, she zoomed up into the air away from him. He did not expect this and crashed head-first into the ground.

Focusing on a dead tree with twisted branches on it, Emer let the remaining Bloodclaw gain on her and then barrel-rolled through the tree. The Bloodclaw tried to do the same, but he tangled himself in the branches, shredding parts of his wings.

"Yes!" Emer exclaimed. She spread her wings, flying up so high she could see the tops of the gray-white mountains.

"Okay! There's the cave! We'll be there sooner than you can say—"

"BLOODCLAW!" Gabby screamed.

"What?" An angry roar erupted as a furious Bloodclaw blocked her way. "I thought I trapped you in a tree!" Emer yelled as she swerved away from the Bloodclaw, blood dripping from its tattered wings.

She dived down into a hidden passage. It was a narrow canyon with a small opening at its end. "Just hold on tight," she reassured her passengers. "We'll be safe soon!"

"As long as we don't get crushed!" Paris yelled as a crumbling noise filled the air. Stones began to fall behind them, crushing the Bloodclaw chasing after them.

A rockslide? Those never happen here! Emer thought.

"You guys are going to have to trust me right now!" Emer said."Let go of my scales!"

"WHAT! ARE YOU CRAZY?" Paris yelled.

"Just trust me!"

Raider, Paris, and Gabby paused and then let go. They

slid off her back. She wrapped her wings around them and then curled into a ball and catapulted through the hole. All of them were screaming.

"Oof!"

"Ow!"

"Ouch!"

Emer tumbled into the cave, not daring to even look up. "I think we're safe."

"Emer? What are you doing?" a noble voice asked.

She looked up. Panic swept over her.

She had landed in the Meeting Room of the Bluescale cave.

Only all the council dragons were in there.

As well as the chief.

CHAPTER 7

FACING THE COUNCIL

Emer could not believe what she had done. She thought she had gotten her friends out of danger, but she had just led them into huge trouble. How would the Bluescales react to her bringing three humans into their home?

Thankfully, they didn't question why her wings looked as if they were covering up something.

"Emer? What are you doing in here?" Majesty demanded, rising to his full height. He was the largest of all the Bluescales and had the horns to match. His midnight-blue scales glistened in the sunlight that leaked through the small hole above them. While other dragons had yellow-gold chest plates, his gleamed of pure gold. He had the aura of a leader and was usually a kind and just chief.

He didn't look kind at this moment, however.

"Oh . . ." Emer thought quickly, her mind weaving a story together. "Well, I was cruising around the mountains

when there was a rockslide. I rolled into a ball and tumbled through the light hole."

Majesty examined her. "Emer, you sustained a wing tear! And hurt your toes! And there's dust all over your scales!"

"I had to fight against the Bloodclaws beforehand. Then Vladmir fixed me, and then I went out for a flight." She grinned sheepishly.

"Emer! You should have been resting! Why in the name of the Greatwing would you practice your flight after you were hurt?" Majesty looked at her, disbelief and worry in his eyes.

"Whoopsy doo!" Paris said, her voice shaking as she wobbled out from under Bella's wings and then collapsed to the ground.

All the dragons in the room gasped.

"EMER! How dare you bring a lowly human into the Bluescale cave!" Knifeclaw yelled, storming his way over to her. She did not want to pick a fight with him. His scar-covered blue-gray scales, dull cracked chest plates, broken horn, and scarred right eye said it all.

"Knifeclaw!" Majesty yelled. "Leave her alone! She most likely has a logical reason for bringing a human into our cave!"

"Actually, three." Emer winced and raised her wings, revealing Gabby and Raider. They both looked pale from Bella's wild entrance.

The dragons gasped. Yells rang up from the council members.

"Kill the humans!"

"No! Save them! Some humans are good!"

"Why? They've taken our land and killed our kind!"

"The Greatwing wants us to treat creatures the same as we treat ourselves!"

"They're only children!"

"They'll grow up into true humans!"

"Why does it even matter? They're not warriors!" one dragon yelled. "They'll just turn out to be like the humans that have become bloated bubbles that hobble around, continuously looking at flat rectangles!"

"Or they'll be like those humans that don't wear their clothes correctly, like they're trying to attract mates to them! And they'll speak in peculiar abbreviations and misuse words to sound 'cooler'!"

"Some humans their age are quite strong!"

"Oxen are smarter than some of those strong humans! Brains are better than brawn!"

"What does it matter?"

"Humans have ruined themselves!"

"SILENCE!" Majesty flared his wings in aggravation.

All the dragons became silent.

"Now," he said, glaring at the council members, "I know that it has been more than four hundred years since we have had any interaction with the human species, except for Emer. However, maybe we can ask them questions of why they are here and how they wound up interacting with us dragons in the first place. You there!" Majesty pointed at Raider. "What caused you to come here today?"

Raider gulped, looking paler than before. Emer felt sorry that Majesty picked him; Raider hated to speak to a crowd.

"Well, you see—"

Paris interrupted. "We were working in the library when our friend Bella glanced out the window! She was like, 'Oh, my gosh, you guys have gotta run!' and she ran away really fast! Raider was all worried and like, 'Oh no, what is wrong?' and then smoke and growls filled the air, and then the roof collapsed! This really big, red, terrible dragon came down and was like, 'HISSS!' When Gabby saw that awful dragon, she was like, 'Oh, DEAR!' and fainted, and Raider was like, 'I'm a chicken, I'll hide under the table,' but I was the brave one, and I was like, 'Get over here, you overgrown beast!' I hurled two bricks at it, but it grabbed me with its smelly talons and hurled me into a cage—"

"Oh, great—do we have to hear the part about me hiding under the table?" Raider scowled.

"And the part about me fainting?" Gabby asked as well.

"Shhh! Let her talk." Majesty smiled. Emer looked around and realized that most of the other council members seemed interested in the story Paris was telling.

"And so this blue dragon with an emerald on her chest came over and beat the stuffing out of the red dragon and slammed her fist through his chest or something, and I was like, 'HOLY COW, THAT WAS AWESOME!' and Gabby was like, 'OH GAWSH!' and Raider was like, 'Wow, that was AMAZING!'"

"I did not say that!" Raider said.

"Uh-huh. And this other dragon came over to Emer, and they just stared at each other for a long time, and then this red dragon with a cracked horn and really creepy white scarred eye grabbed us and brought us back to a dark, creepy cave—"

"Scareye? He's the one who captured you?" Majesty asked, his voice now serious.

No wonder I thought he looked familiar. Emer recalled the way the Bloodclaw who'd stolen the cage had looked and acted. *He and Scareye are the same dragon! Oh, how I hate him.*

"And then this dragon named Demonheart tried to talk with us—"

All the dragons gasped.

"Demonheart!" Majesty exclaimed, his wings flaring out at the mention of the name. "He talked to you?"

"More like told us we might be part of something called 'The Foretelling.' And Scareye, his crazy swearing assistant, investigated us."

Now the council was jabbering away to each other.

"But it gets better!" Paris yelled, getting their attention. "A dragon named Emer, the dragon who had tried to save us earlier, chopped down a stalactite and saved us! We rode out on her back and flew away from three Bloodclaws and a rockslide, and she tumbled into here and made me collapse until you told Mr. Shy-Guy over here to tell a story!"

"Thank you for explaining that all for me," Raider whispered to Paris. She nodded, grinning gleefully.

Majesty paced across his Ledge. "Demonheart captured them . . . said they were The Chosen Ones . . . Emer saved them . . ." he mumbled to himself. Emer's friends seemed to take notice that all the council members were staring eagerly at Majesty.

Suddenly, a pair of white-and-gold wings swept over them and landed on Majesty's Ledge.

"Who's that?" Gabby asked.

"That's Vladmir," Emer whispered to her. "He's the wise dragon here. If you're sick, injured, dealing with a struggle, or just want to learn, see him."

Vladmir and Majesty stared at each other for a long time, tilting their heads occasionally or moving their wings.

"What are they doing?" Raider asked.

"Yeah, why are they just staring at each other?" Paris asked.

"They're telecommunicating," Emer told them.

"What?" all three children said at the same time.

"Yes, some dragons telecommunicate, like Bluescales," she said. "Other dragons, like the Bloodclaws, cannot. We do it so humans and animals can't hear us."

"Cool!" Paris exclaimed.

"Freaky," Raider said.

"Oh, gosh." Gabby sighed.

Vladmir looked at the four of them and then flew down to them. He approached them with slight caution. Emer's friends backed away.

"What the heck is he doing?!" Paris asked, sounding worried.

"Don't worry. You can trust him." Emer gave her friends a reassuring smile.

Vladmir looked at them. Then he said, "The boy and sun-haired girl are different colored sapphires. The earth-haired girl is a ruby."

Majesty's shocked face stared at the children. The rest of the council seemed just as surprised.

Vladmir looked at Emer's friends even more closely.

It's like he's staring into their souls, she thought.

A long silence filled the cave. No one spoke. No one dared to even move.

"They have it."

Shocked silence.

"They do?" Majesty uttered, a mixture of shock, surprise, and even happiness in his voice.

"They have it."

The dragons rejoiced.

Cheers filled the room as no one had ever heard; the happiness of a dragon is highly contagious. Happy cries echoed around, and dragons hugged each other. Some dragons even threw paperwork into the air like confetti and lit it on fire. Majesty's smile and good energy radiated around the room. Vladmir smiled his kind, knowing smile even more brightly than ever.

Emer had never seen any dragons this joyous.

"But how are they The Chosen Ones if they're humans?" Knifeclaw asked. "If they're humans, they're powerless."

Vladmir turned his head at the only dragon that wasn't rejoicing. "Honestly, if they have the Dragon Spirit, it means they're part of The Foretelling. And the humans will solve the problem in their own way."

"Wait, what?" Paris asked.

"What are you making us do?" Gabby asked.

Vladmir smiled at them. "Younglings, you stick out from those other humans who bring disgrace to their kind. You are meant to achieve great things. But first, you have to solve a riddle."

"A riddle? I should be able to figure that out," Raider said. "Oooh, a riddle," Paris said. "Oh no, not a riddle," Gabby groaned. "Here is the riddle: Listen carefully," Vladmir said.

"Found on a cold and stormy night,
Now with us, helping our fight
Though she's not with us in the day
Her loyalty is here to stay
But she's special, different, exotic, I say,
She's seen by the world in two different ways.
To us, she's a warrior, brave and strong,
Defending the good, destroying the wrong,
But to humans, she's seen as a friend,
A kind helper, staying to the end.
But by using your heart instead of your eyes
You can see past her disguise
If you can see past her different form
Tell me tomorrow, in the morn
Answer the riddle, this I vow
That this creature exists. Just how
Can a person, this special someone,
Have the power of two creatures in one?"

"How the heck am I supposed to solve that?" Paris exclaimed, frustrated.

"You will know when it is the time," Vladmir said. He turned to Majesty. "Let them rest. Find them somewhere to sleep and think. This riddle is very important for the fate of our kind, as well as the fate of the world."

"The meeting is adjourned!" Majesty proclaimed, and the stunned dragons left the cave. Emer glanced down at her friends.

"Don't worry. Everything will turn out fine," Emer reassured.

"Are you sure?" Gabby asked.

"I'm positive."

"Good." Gabby smiled at her.

Emer smiled back, but in her head, she was worried. *Will everything really be all right?*

CHAPTER

SOLVING THE RIDDLE

Raider was thinking about the riddle.

A warrior who is a great friend.

That has got to be Bella.

But how? It doesn't make any scientific sense. Humans, mammals, cannot transform into dragons, which are reptiles. Or can they? Are they just switching the image that someone sees? Or is it a genetic mutation that allows the DNA in her body to grow into the form of a dragon and then shrink back to human form? It's so weird.

"And here is where I stay," Emer's voice broke his train of thought. "My home."

"But where are you during the day?" Raider blurted out, remembering that part from the riddle.

Emer glared at him. "I explore during the day. Quit snooping." She shoved open the door to her room and then stomped inside.

Paris stopped Raider. "You really shouldn't make her angry," she warned.

"Why?"

"Did you see how the dragons had mixed feelings about humans? We don't know if she feels that way about us."

"But she saved us! Doesn't that prove she likes us?"

Paris sighed, shaking her head. "Just don't annoy her, okay? I'm trying to become friends with her." She walked off, beginning to talk to Gabby, who was watching them.

Well, they can't see who she is, he thought. He followed them into the room. *But what if it's not Bella, and I totally screw up? Then it'll be a mess.*

I'll just keep an eye out.

"Wow!" Gabby exclaimed, interrupting Raider's thoughts. He entered Emer's room and was surprised at what he saw.

Unlike the other dull-gray Bluescale rooms he had glanced into as he passed them, this room had tiny wildflowers in carved-out rocks sitting in little niches around the room. Hearing water, he looked around and spotted a small waterfall trickling into a stone reservoir. An orange crystal like the ones he had seen along the hallways and in Bluescale rooms was attached to the wall.

"Ooh, look at this!" Gabby said. She was looking at a bright hammock, full of neon colors.

That's different, Raider thought. *In all the other caves I glanced into, they slept on stone slabs. Why is Emer so different?*

"COWABUNGA!" Paris yelled, charging at the hammock and leaping into it. It swung back and forth as if it was in torrential winds.

"Hey!" Emer yelled, dashing over to Paris's chaos. "There are other hammocks over there that you can destroy." She pointed into the corner, where three small hammocks hung. Paris immediately leaped off Emer's swinging hammock and collapsed into one of them, claiming it as her own.

Raider walked over to his hammock when something caught on his foot. He stumbled but managed to regain his balance. *What was that?* he wondered, looking back at the floor.

It was a notebook that resembled his spiral-bound notebook, only the cover was leather, and the spirals were leather laces. Raider picked it up with care, slid his hand across the smooth leather cover, and opened the notebook.

Drawings of many different dragons greeted him on every page. He recognized some of them from stories, but there were many he had never seen before.

So Emer likes to draw, just like Bella, he pondered. *That's another point of proof.*

"Wow, those are amazing!" Gabby exclaimed, looking at the drawings. "Hey, is it just me, or do these drawings seem somewhat similar to Bella's drawings?"

"What are you doing with my notebook?" Emer asked, startling Raider. He noted there was slight fear in her voice as she snatched the notebook from his hands.

"There's no need to be mad!" Gabby said. "We were just admiring your drawings and how they look similar to one of our friends' drawings."

Did only he notice it, or did panic spread across her face for a mere second?

"Oh," she said. Raider picked up hints of nervousness in her voice. "It's probably just a coincidence."

"Okay."

"Hello?" an unfamiliar voice interrupted.

It may have been unfamiliar to Raider, but Emer seemed to know immediately who it was. She dashed over to him and greeted him with enthusiasm.

"Stonehorn! Hi!" she said.

"Well, hello, Emer." He smiled at her.

Raider inspected the dragon. His scales were a pale blue; his horns and claws were a bright yellow. He did not have any wounds at all as far as Raider could tell. Stonehorn was only a little bigger than Emer, so he probably wasn't that old.

"Hey, everyone here! This is Stonehorn! He's a Cave Helper!" Emer introduced him.

"Hi! I'm Gabby," Gabby said. "And this is Paris."

"What's up?" Paris said.

"And this is Raider."

"Hello." Raider smiled.

"So, these are The Chosen Ones?" Stonehorn asked Emer with awe.

"According to the council, yes."

"Oh. Wow." Stonehorn looked at them. "Well, I brought some food for the children. Fire-roasted buffalo drizzled with a sweet syrup made of strawberries and prickly pears!"

"Yum!" Paris said with glee.

Mealtime passed, and the children discussed the riddle they were supposed to figure out. However, they did not get very far.

"Raider, why do you keep bringing Bella into this whole mess?" Paris shouted at him.

"Yeah, you've brought her up, like, ten times now," Gabby said, annoyed.

"Well, she might be in the riddle," Raider mumbled sheepishly.

"She ran away! She betrayed us!" Paris said. Raider wouldn't be surprised if any dragons nearby stuck their heads in Emer's room just to see what was going on.

He also saw Emer wince at what Paris said.

"You know what? It's been a long day. A lot has happened, I'm really tired, and my stomach is full of buffalo and strawberry–prickly pear sauce! So I'm going to bed!" Paris leaped up into one of the three hammocks Emer had set up for them. It swung with a stormy violence. "Good night! And don't let all those dragons bite!" she barked in a huff and then was quiet.

Gabby and Raider stared at each other. It felt awkward when Paris ran off in a mad fit.

"Do you want to keep trying to figure out this riddle?" Raider asked.

"I'm sorry, Raider, but I'm really tired as well." Gabby yawned. "Maybe tomorrow." She crawled into her hammock, which stayed still as she lay down in it.

"Good night, Raider."

Great, Raider thought. *Now Gabby and Paris are asleep, and I'm the only person who wants to figure out this crazy riddle. I know Emer is a warrior whose enemies frown when they see her and that Bella is sometimes looked down upon in school just because she likes dragons, but I can't see how the heck it would even be possible.*

Raider would have crawled into his hammock had he not recalled something Bella had said.

"You'll see me by your heart."

Everything that had happened that day flooded through his mind. He recalled everything Emer had done: how she had come back to save them; how she had smiled at them when she knew they were safe; how concerned she was when the council was talking; the difference between her room and the other dragons' rooms; her drawings; and how similar she was to Bella.

And Raider knew at that moment how to prove that his theory was correct.

He recalled a memory from a time at school. He had dumped water on Bella's head to tease her. He had thought she would be mad at him, but she hadn't been.

Raider grabbed a stone flowerpot and dumped out the flower and dirt. He dipped it into the water reservoir and, when it was full, crept ever so quietly over to Emer, who was sound asleep in her hammock.

Just remember that it's Bella, he thought, nervous.

Poke.

Poke.

"Hrmm, who's there?" Emer grumbled, shuffling around in her hammock.

"Just Raider. And I have a gift for you!" He threw the water on her. Sputtering, she sat up, which caused the hammock to sway. Emer lost her balance and flopped out of the hammock onto the floor with an immense THUD. She stood up to her full height, which Raider had calculated to be somewhere around ten feet.

Emer, to the common eye, seemed to be upset. But Raider could tell she was trying her hardest to suppress a smile, and her eyes were twinkling with mischief and happiness.

"So, you dare try to upset a dragon, do you?" she said. Her voice was a combination of forced anger, cleverness, and happiness. "You dare try to get me wet? You dare poke ME?" She approached him.

Raider backed up as close to his hammock as he could, but he could not escape this Bluescale. Emer stared straight into his eyes. It felt as if she was staring into his soul.

"Well, you know what?"

"What?" Raider asked, wondering what would happen.

"I'm going to poke you back!" Before he knew what was happening, her talon was poking him in the stomach to make him laugh.

"Ack! Stop it, Emer! Emer!" he said between laughs, eventually laughing so hard that he fell to the ground.

SPLOOSH! Emer doused him with water!

Raider was dripping wet! He sat up, the cold water freezing his skin and shaking his bones.

Emer sat down next to him, snickering at his suffering. "You're all wet!" she laughed.

Annoyed, Raider flicked water at her. She blocked it with her wing.

"Hey, Mr. Wet Man, you want me to dry you off?" she asked. "I can dry you with fire or air."

"Air, please. I don't want to be burned with fire."

Emer beat her wings, and air whished onto him, drying his skin in seconds.

"Thanks," he said.

Emer's tail waved back and forth. "Why did you dump water on me? And poke me?" she asked.

"Just because."

"There's a logical reason for everything. Just tell me."

"I just did it for the heck of it!"

"Okay, then." Emer walked over to the light crystal. "It just reminded me of something."

"What?" Raider asked.

"Something that someone has done to me before."

"Really?"

"Yes." She hesitated. Emer gazed at the floor. "I enjoyed what you did," she admitted in a whisper.

Shock and happiness filled him. Raider knew that Bella would say something like that!

Emer touched the strange glowing crystal on the wall. The light emitting from it disappeared, leaving the cave in darkness.

"Good night, Raider."

Raider climbed into his hammock and stared up at the ceiling. He liked the glowing spots resembling stars.

Raider knew his theory was true, and it was the answer to the riddle. It wasn't a strange guess anymore. It was a fact he knew.

Emer and Bella were the same person.

"Good night, Bella," he whispered just as he drifted off into sleep.

CHAPTER 9

THE RIDDLE'S ANSWER

"Good night, Bella."

Those words were stuck in Emer's mind. *Did he figure it out? Does he know the answer to the riddle? To my secret?* But part of her mind doubted that thought. *No, he only met me earlier this year. Paris and Gabby are more likely to know the answer . . . but they haven't been pestering me as Raider has . . . and he is the class intellectual . . .*

It was very early the next morning. A sleepy Emer was scrubbing her scales clean from the previous day's battles. She growled, her tail thrashing with frustration, sending water from the hot spring everywhere. Sinking her head halfway into the water, Emer sighed. *I just need to relax.*

"Emer?"

"Aaaagh!" Emer turned around, startled, her wings flaring. The water flew onto Vladmir, who was standing above her.

SPLOOSH!

"Oops." Emer cringed.

"It's alright, Emer," Vladmir said. "Besides, you must be washing your scales from yesterday's adventure."

"Yes." Emer relaxed into the steaming water, too hot for humans, but just right for dragons.

Vladmir looked at her. "You're nervous about the riddle, aren't you?"

She looked up, startled. "How did you know?"

"You're jittery. And you look nervous."

Emer sighed. "I am. I just—"

"There's no need to be scared." Vladmir smiled at her. "Everything will turn out fine in the end." Vladmir walked out of the hot spring room.

But will it? Emer wondered, lifting herself out of the warm water. *I guess I'll just have to wait and see.*

She shook herself off and walked out of the hot spring room. Emer passed down a number of crystal-lit hallways, at first small and narrow with scarcely any rooms and then large and wide with many living spaces, leading to the Meeting Room.

Oh, great. The entryway was crowded with Bluescales! Emer knew the only way she could get through was to squeeze past them. So she did.

"Oof!"

"Hey!"

"Watch it!"

"Sorry!" Emer apologized. "But I've got to be here on time!"

"So do we!" a Bluescale yelled. But Emer could not have cared less. She was already flying up to Majesty's Ledge. He had been waiting there for her. Majesty's dark-blue scales shone even brighter than before.

"Ah, Emer, you made it," Majesty said, smiling.

"Yes," Emer replied. "Where are my frien—I mean, The Ones?"

Majesty chuckled. "They're over there." He pointed his wing at the three children standing with Stonehorn.

"Thanks!" Emer spread her wings and glided down to her friends.

"Ah! You're here," Stonehorn said. "I should get going now. It's very chaotic out there. I've never seen activity like this!"

"If you think this is chaos, you should see a battle between enemy forces," Emer said.

Stonehorn looked at her. "You've got me there. It must be terrible."

"It is."

"I must get going! Good-bye!" Stonehorn flew off.

"Hey, Emer," Gabby said. "How old is that Stonehorn dragon?"

"He's eighteen summers old."

"And how old are you?"

"Thirteen springs."

"Oh."

"One of our friends is thirteen!" Raider said.

"Raider!" Paris exclaimed. "Stop bringing Bella into this whole mess!"

"Raider! Gabby! Paris! Shhh! Majesty is going to speak!" Emer shushed them. They became quiet and listened.

"Fellow Bluescales, whether part of the council, part of the clan, a dragon who believes in The Foretelling, or you just want to know what is happening here, I greet you with warmth." Majesty walked along his Ledge.

"Dragons used to rule the earth. We used to soar the blue skies, roam the land, feel the grass and flowers and trees, and feel the sun giving energy to our scales. All dragons worked together, whether small or big, fire breather or ice breather, a dragon of the sky or a dragon of the earth. Dragons of all different kinds worked together to keep each other safe and happy."

Emer noticed some Bluescales looking happy or even sad at what Majesty said.

"But all was not well. Strange creatures called humans feared us and sent men clad in armor to end our lives. Their only reason for existence seemed to be to torture us dragons. To make matters worse, four hundred years ago, the Bloodclaws rose. They attacked all of us, splitting our connections with different kinds of dragons and stealing our most precious artifacts, including the Dark Energy Crystal. They captured every creature who dared to even stand up to them, torturing them for the fun of it, letting them die slow deaths." Some of the dragons growled at this, even spitting out fire in anger. Emer glanced down at her friends. They looked horrified at what Majesty was saying.

"With the humans' fear and yearning to kill us, and the threat of the Bloodclaws, all the dragons existing in the world had no other option than to go into hiding, whether it be hiding in caves or gaining camouflage powers or developing the power to only be seen by dragons, animals, or humans with pure hearts. Even the heartless, soulless Bloodclaws realized the humans were a greater danger than they were and went into hiding. All the dragons vanished from human eye, and, after only ten years, we were dubbed 'not real.' We had no hope for the future. Life was miserable."

"It would still be that way, had it not been for The Foretelling," Vladmir interrupted, walking out of the crowd, standing underneath Majesty's Ledge. "A dragon managed to hear a message from the Celestials. They said that four warriors—one green, one blue, one yellow, and one red—would rise from the lowest race of the earth to help the dragons in their greatest time of need. Many were hopeful after they heard this, but nothing happened. Some began to give up hope. Some were without faith from the beginning. But today, four hundred years from when the Bloodclaws took control, we believe we have found The Chosen Ones."

Most of the dragons cheered, especially the ones from the council. But as Emer watched, she noticed some of the dragons looking doubtful. Knifeclaw was one of them.

"Emer!" Majesty yelled. "Bring The Chosen Ones here!"

"Okay," she said. Emer motioned for her friends to follow her. They did, and Emer walked over to Vladmir.

"These children have the Dragon Spirit!" Majesty announced. The Bluescales cheered again. "As told in The Foretelling, the four warriors will have it, even though they will look as if they do not!"

"And they were given a riddle," Vladmir said. "They were to know the answer today."

Emer glanced down at her friends. Gabby looked nervous. Paris looked as if she couldn't care less. Raider looked determined yet calm.

"Earth-haired girl! What is the answer to the riddle?" Vladmir asked.

Gabby gulped. "I-I don't know," she mumbled. "I didn't get it."

"It was very confusing!" Paris objected. "I didn't get it, either! All I could get from the poem is that it's about a girl with two forms who you can see with your heart. You can't see with your heart!"

"So neither of you has figured out the riddle," Vladmir stated.

"I figured it was connected to Emer in some way, but it was just a confusing piece of baloney," Paris huffed, crossing her arms.

Majesty glared at Vladmir; Emer could tell they were telecommunicating.

"But there is still the boy," Vladmir said. "The boy has not answered yet."

"I know the answer!" Raider's voice rang out.

Silence filled the cave.

Emer felt her heart hammering in her chest. She felt sick.

"You know the answer?" Majesty asked, shocked.

"Yes. It's about a girl—one who makes frequent trips between the dragons and the humans. The dragons call her a brave warrior, and the humans call her a good friend. Even though she is seen in two different ways, she is the same person."

Paris and Gabby stared at Raider, astounded.

"And I've learned what the riddle means," Raider continued. "We three see the person from the riddle. That person is Bella. And the Bluescales see the dragon from the riddle. That dragon is Emer."

"What are you saying?" Gabby asked.

"I'm saying that Emer and Bella are the same being."

The dragons in the crowd gasped, surprised that this human could solve the riddle.

"What?" Gabby exclaimed.

"Prove it," Paris said.

"Emer came to rescue us when we were in trouble. She rescued us twice. She did everything she could to keep us safe. She stayed by us in the cave. She knows all our names. And she liked it when I dumped water on her. Only Bella would do this. They are the same being!" Raider explained.

"Emer?" Gabby asked. "Is this true?"

Emer, knowing she couldn't hide her secret any longer, sighed. "Yes, I am Bella."

Gabby gasped, immediately believing her.

Paris, however, was doubtful. "How do I know you're telling the truth? Tell me something only my friend Bella would know."

"You have a fear of dragonflies," Emer said.

Paris's jaw dropped. "You're Bella."

"Young boy," Vladmir said, walking over to Raider, "you figured out the riddle. You saw with your heart. Therefore, you will be granted a great reward." Vladmir touched

Raider's forehead with the tip of his talon, careful to not hurt the small human. "You have been seen your whole life as a human when a wonderful gift lies unknown inside of you."

Emer noticed light beginning to emit from Vladmir's talon.

"Let the Dragon Spirit in you be awakened!" Vladmir proclaimed. "Saphir, I command you to rise!" With those words, bright white light filled the whole cave. Dragons covered their eyes with their wings. Paris and Gabby covered their eyes. Emer covered hers as well.

What is Vladmir doing to him? Emer wondered, concerned about what was happening.

The light began to fade away. Emer looked up.

She could not believe what she saw.

A dragon stood before her. He had sapphire-blue scales as well as yellow-gold chest plates, claws, and large ram horns. He looked like any other Bluescale, only he had a sapphire on his chest and little blue gems on the end of his tail.

To Emer's disbelief, it was another Dralerian.

Not just any Dralerian, however.

It was her friend Raider.

Raider gazed at one claw. His eyes widened with shock. He looked at his new tail, his wings, and his sharp, golden talons.

"I'm . . . I'm a dragon."

The Bluescales cheered. They cried, "The warriors have risen! The warriors have risen! The Dark Age will soon be gone!"

Emer smiled at the sight before her. All the dragons were happy. Even Knifeclaw had a smile on his face.

Suddenly, pain flew through her handlike front talons. Paris had deliberately stomped on them.

"OW!" She pulled her claw up, rubbing it. She looked down.

Paris and Gabby were standing close to her, glaring at her.

"Bella or Emer," Paris said, "we need to talk."

CHAPTER 10

TO TRUST AGAIN

"How could you keep a secret like that from us?!" Paris yelled.

Emer, Gabby, and Paris were back in Emer's room at the Bluescale cave.

"Why didn't you tell us?" Gabby asked, her voice both sad and angry at the same time. "Didn't you trust us?"

Emer was silent. She placed her right claw over her emerald. With a bright flash of light, she was back in her human form.

"See? See! That's just the point right there!" Paris yelled, gesturing to Bella. "You have this ability to transform into a dragon. A dragon, of all creatures! No wonder you liked them so much! They were your family, not us!"

Bella sighed, close to tears. "There's a logical reason I didn't tell you!" she cried.

"Why?" Paris yelled, nearly screaming with anger. "Because you were simply too pigheaded and arrogant with your little dragon friends to even care about us? If you were our friend, you would have told us!"

"I couldn't tell you!" Bella shouted, louder than Paris.

"WHY?!" Paris screamed.

CREAK. The door to Bella's room opened. Stonehorn stuck his head in.

"Emer, I'm ready to—" He glanced down at them. Paris had yelled so much her face was red. Gabby was depressed. Bella was doing her best to not cry.

"Not now, Stonehorn," Bella croaked, her voice shaky.

"Oh . . . oh . . . trust issues . . . I see." Stonehorn slowly backed away. "I'll . . . just . . . wait out here . . . heh-heh . . . sorry." He zoomed out of the room, shutting the door with a SLAM.

The three children stared at the door. *Leave it to Stonehorn to enter at the wrong time,* Bella thought to herself.

"Why didn't you tell us, you—" Paris began to yell, but Gabby stopped her. She grabbed Paris's shoulders and glared at her, one of the only times Bella had seen Gabby like this.

"Bella is our friend," Gabby said, staying calm but still a little angry. "Even though she didn't tell us a really big secret she had, she has no right to be yelled at like this." She looked over at Bella, who was shaking. "If you had a secret this big, Paris, you wouldn't tell anyone, would you?"

Paris looked at Gabby, confused. "I'd tell everybody," she said casually.

Gabby sighed. "No, you wouldn't. Let's just listen to our friend and see why she kept this secret hidden. Okay?"

Paris huffed out a sigh but turned to face Bella. "Fine. Bella, why didn't you tell us you were an all-powerful dragon warrior?"

"Because you would have thought I was crazy," Bella replied. "You would have thought I was out of my mind, only imagining crazy things. And if you had known beforehand and believed that I am half-dragon, you would have sent the police, FBI, SWAT team, and everyone else to capture me and my dragon friends for scientific investigation. I didn't want that. I wanted you to trust me, and I wanted to stay friends with you."

"But why?" Paris asked angrily. "Wouldn't you have wanted to stay with your cool and awesome dragon friends?"

Bella smiled a weak smile. "Because you three are awesome friends. You're even cooler than the dragons I live with part of the time."

"Really?" Paris asked, astounded.

"Aw." Gabby smiled, tears filling her eyes. "That's so sweet! Group hug!" she cried, and she hugged Bella. Bella hugged Gabby back.

"Oh, you big saps!" Paris smiled and joined the hug.

"Wait a sec," Gabby said, releasing Bella and Paris. "That's why you ran! The Bloodclaws were attacking, and you—"

"I was planning on transforming into a dragon and then going back to protect you. I needed to be in dragon form in order to do any good. I'm surprised you didn't need my help."

"We defended ourselves pretty well," Gabby said. "Just ask Paris."

"I threw two bricks at the Bloodclaw!" Paris exclaimed.

"I have a question," Gabby said. "Did Demonheart try to capture us because we're part of 'The Foretelling' thing?"

"Yeah," Paris joined in.

Bella thought a minute. "Demonheart probably figured out that you three might be part of The Foretelling before the Bluescales did. So they sent the attack on the school, only capturing you three, and they intended on burning everyone else who had seen the attack."

"Oh! That's why they tried to burn down the school!" Paris exclaimed.

"But they didn't!" Gabby said. "The Bluescales came, as well as you, and stopped them from totally burning the school and hurting the kids!"

"Except for you two and Raider." Bella frowned. "You managed to fall into Demonheart and Scareye's grasp."

"We would have escaped if you hadn't made it," Paris said boldly.

"No, you wouldn't have." Bella scowled. "Demonheart would have killed you, part of The Foretelling or not. He makes it nearly impossible to enter or exit his lair. You never would have found your way out. And if Demonheart hadn't killed you, one of the other Bloodclaws would have."

"But then how did you enter, hmm?" Paris asked. "How did you figure out how to get in?"

Bella smiled, knowing her friends had caught her there. "That's another story for another day."

"Hello? Emer? May I come in now?" Stonehorn asked from behind her door.

I completely forgot about Stonehorn! Bella thought. "Yeah, hang on a second!" she yelled. She touched her hand to her heart. Bright light flashed around the cave, and once again, she became Emer.

"Could you give me a warning the next time you do that?" Paris grumbled, rubbing her eyes.

"Wow, that's so amazing," Gabby said in awe.

"You can come in, Stonehorn!" Emer called out.

The pale-blue Bluescale peeked his head in the room. "No yelling? No screaming?" he muttered. "Good."

"Stonehorn is going to teach you about the Bluescales and the Bluescale cave," Emer told her friends.

"Wait a sec," Gabby said. "Something just occurred to me. Why did Raider get the ability to transform into a dragon and Paris and I are still normal humans?"

"Yeah, I want to be a dragon-human warrior!" Paris said.

"Raider got his Dralerian powers from answering the riddle correctly, and I guess Vladmir thought he was ready," Emer said.

"But will we ever earn the ability to transform?" Gabby asked.

"I would assume so, whenever you're ready," Emer said. "You are The Chosen Ones, after all, and you have the Dragon Spirit, so I would expect you to become a Dralerian."

"What day will that be?" Gabby asked.

"Tomorrow!" Paris exclaimed.

"It's whenever Vladmir decides you're ready. I'm not in control of it," Emer said.

"Oh, okay," Gabby said.

"Why can't I have it now?" Paris asked.

"Because you're not ready yet!" Emer said. "One of those steps to prove that you're ready is to study the Bluescale cave with Stonehorn!"

"Oh!" Paris said. "I'll do that, then!"

"Good." Emer smiled at her friends. "I'll see you two later!"

"Bye, Bella! Or Emer!"

"Just call me Emer when I'm in dragon form!" she called back.

"Bye, Emer!"

With that, Emer walked away from her room, hoping her friends would continue to trust her like before.

CHAPTER 11

DRAGON ATTACK!

Emer was walking down the empty hallway, her talons sliding across the smooth stone floor. *Hmm, what should I do next?* she wondered.

"Ah, Emer! Just the dragon I was looking for!"

"Hi, Vladmir!" Emer said.

"Emer, would you do a favor for me?"

"Sure. What?"

"Would you teach Saphir how to fly?"

It took her a second to remember who Saphir was, but once she remembered, she couldn't forget. Saphir was Raider's dragon name.

"Definitely! Oh, how did you transform Raider into a Dralerian?" she asked, filled with eagerness. "Was he always a Dralerian or what?"

Vladmir chuckled. "He was always a human. However, he had the Dragon Spirit. This could enable someone with advanced powers to grant him the qualities of a Dralerian."

"You have advanced powers?" Emer asked, shocked.

Vladmir only smiled at this. "That's a question for another day. Go find your friend. He will be waiting." With those words, Vladmir walked away, leaving Emer to find her friend.

Now, where is he? Emer thought to herself, glancing into empty rooms and down hallways.

"Oh, that's cool!"

She knew that voice belonged to Saphir. She peeked into the small room where she had heard the voice. There sat the Dralerian Saphir, reading a book aloud.

Emer got an idea. A devious idea. The kind that makes your mouth curve into a devilish grin.

She silently crept into the room. Had she been in human form, she would have been about as stealthy as an angry cat clawing a human. But she was in her dragon form and was creeping along as quietly, no, more quietly than a mouse. She made sure her claws did not clack, her tail did not swish, her wings did not whoosh. She sneaked closer and closer to him, silently, stealthily, flawlessly. And once that was done . . .

She pounced.

"DRAGON ATTAAAAAAAAAACK!" she yelled, diving down at him.

He looked up, startled. "WHAT THE—" he managed to exclaim, but he was interrupted as Emer tackled him. The book he was reading flew through the air. The two of

them tumbled across the floor until they rammed into a wall. CRASH! They crumpled to the floor.

"Ha-ha, very funny, Emer," Saphir said while sitting up, sarcasm in his voice.

"You have to admit it; I did scare you."

"Was that revenge for my dumping water on you?"

"No, that was just for the heck of it." Emer stood up. "Come on, Saphir, we have work to do. Follow me!" She walked out of the small room.

"Hey, wait up!" Saphir soon caught up to her.

"So," Emer asked, "what do you think of being a—"

"Oops!" Saphir tripped on a small rock and fell to the ground.

"You're not used to this, are you?"

"Erg." He pulled himself back up. "Not exactly."

"Don't worry. You'll get used to it." Emer smiled at her friend.

Saphir shook his tail and began to walk forward with caution. "So, what is this Dragon Spirit thing that caused me to become a dragon-human?"

"You mean a Dralerian?"

"Yeah."

"The Dragon Spirit is a very special energy that's found in dragons, Dralerians, and a very select group of humans that believe in dragons," Emer explained.

"Okay," Saphir said. "Where are we going?"

"Just out here." Emer beckoned him to follow and walked out of the cave onto the Flight Ledge. Unlike Majes-

ty's Ledge, this was the takeoff and landing spot for dragons granted permission for a free flight.

As Emer glanced around, she knew it would be a perfect day for flying. The sun was shining, there was a slight
breeze, and not a single lost hiker was in sight.

"Wow," Saphir gasped, looking out at the rocky land-
scape. "This is awesome!"

"What we're going to do next will be even more awesome." Emer smiled a clever smile full of mischief.

"What is it?" Saphir asked, hesitant.

"Today, you're going to learn how to fly."

CHAPTER

FLIGHT LESSONS

Saphir still couldn't believe what had happened earlier that day. When the white, elderly Bluescale Vladmir had gently touched his forehead and released all the weird magic stuff (he didn't know what to call it), he felt as if he was almost being burned, being frozen, being pulled apart, being squished, being filled with energy, and being drained of energy all at the same time.

When he realized he was in dragon form, he was shocked. He didn't know what to do or how to be a dragon. After some practice walking on his four legs—which was no easy task—and watching and talking with some of the Bluescales, he caught on.

However, what Emer had just asked him to do was insane. Out of the question. He would not bring his scaly feet off the precious ground.

"No way," he said, and then he turned around to go back to reading. But he realized he wasn't going anywhere.

Saphir looked back. Emer was grasping his tail.

Aw, great. "Emer, I can't fly. Okay?"

"Then what are these things on your back?" She grinned, yanking one of the wings he had ignored the whole time.

"OW! Hey, don't do that!" he hissed, pulling his wings back. "Wait, did I just hiss?"

"Yes, you did."

"Oh, great. What will my parents think of this?" Saphir groaned.

"That's not something we need to worry about now. Come on, Saphir. Just let me teach you." Emer looked at him, that strange, concerned look in her dragon eyes.

Saphir sighed. "Fine. Show me how to fly."

"Yay!" She immediately brightened up. "First, you spread your wings." She spread her wings out. They were bigger than he had thought. He also noticed a strange black mark on one of her wing membranes.

"What's that?" he asked, pointing at the black line.

"Oh, this." She looked down at the mark. "This is a wing tear. Dragons sometimes get them in battle. They really hurt. Mine got stitched up and should be good as new soon." She touched the mark and winced.

"You're teaching me to fly when you know there's a bunch of demon-dragons that roam about in the shadows waiting to shred your wings?" he demanded. "Why?"

"Because you'll be able to escape them faster than if you were to run away," she said sternly.

Emer had a point there. Rolling his eyes, Saphir spread out his wings. They were surprisingly large, yet light and easy to move. His scales glinted in the sunlight like a trove of sapphires and yellow gems.

"Now, all you need to do is leap off the ledge and spread your wings, and you'll fly!" Emer said.

"What!" Saphir exclaimed. "There is no way I would ever jump off a cliff ledge! Ever!"

"You would if there were a Bloodclaw chasing after you," Emer pointed out.

Saphir grumbled. She was right again. "Fine, I'll do it." He walked over to the edge of the ledge, hesitant about what he would do.

Is this really a smart choice? he worried. *Do I really trust what Emer is telling me? Will I actually fly?*

There's only one way I'll find out.

He stuck out his front claw . . .

And stepped off the Flight Ledge.

"AAAAAAAGH!" he screamed, plummeting like a stone, falling down toward the rocks beneath him.

Without thinking, Saphir spread his wings.

WHOOSH!

Saphir's eyes were shut tightly. He heard laughing.

"Emer? Am I dead yet?" he asked, fear in his voice.

She simply laughed. "You're not dead! Open your eyes!"

He slowly opened his eyes, scared of what he might see. But what he saw amazed him.

The evening sun made the mountains beneath him gleam. He had never seen anything like it. He also realized something else.

He was flying.

"Emer! I'm flying!" Saphir looked at his wings to make sure this wasn't a dream. "Look at me!"

She smiled at his excitement. "As exciting as gliding is, you need to know how to really fly."

"Wait, what? Aren't I flying now?" Saphir asked, confused.

"Well, yes, but I mean battle flying. Just trust your instinct and follow me!" She dived down between the rocks below them.

Trust my instinct, he thought. *What instinct?* He gulped and folded his wings, flying down through the mountain pass. As he flapped his wings, he was surprised to find himself flying quite fast.

He watched Emer barrel-roll through a hole in a rock.

Oh, great. How am I going to do that? Saphir slammed his eyes shut, tucked in his wings, and spun through the hole.

He opened his eyes, scared. Realizing he had not crashed to the ground, he whispered a victorious, "I did it!" and returned to flying straight again. Saphir chased after Emer for quite a while, performing sharp turns, loop-de-loops, and even flying upside down to catch up to her, all the while getting better and better.

Emer, who seemed to notice this, veered straight up into the air into the clouds.

Saphir followed in hot pursuit, flying after her. He glanced around the clouds, trying to find where Emer was hiding. His eyes caught a blue flash of movement.

He flew toward the movement through a cloud and caught up to a surprised Emer once again.

She smiled a clever and mischievous smile and then folded back her wings and began to plummet to the ground.

Great, he growled to himself. Then, despite his nervous stomach, he folded himself into a dive. Saphir zoomed downward, a scaly blue bullet chasing after his target. He was traveling so fast the air screamed in his ears, making him unable to hear anything but the roar of the wind.

Emer's wings sliced out, and she veered away from the plateau below her. *Oh, shoot!* Saphir only just realized how close he was to the ground. He spread his large wings, which was hard because the air pressed against him. Saphir slowed himself down, gliding only inches above the ground, but his claw caught on the rock beneath him. Saphir tumbled forward, hitting the dusty ground.

THUD. Emer landed beside him. "Not bad for your first day being a Dralerian," she said in an impressed voice.

Saphir stumbled back to his feet. His whole body hurt from his rough landing. "Thank you," he said. "But why do you keep calling me a Dralerian?"

"That's what a human who can transform into a dragon with the power of a gemstone is called," Emer answered him, pointing at her emerald.

"Wait a sec." Saphir thought. "You have an emerald as your gemstone, and you were born in May, correct?"

"Yes."

"And I was born in September, and I have a sapphire. So does a Dralerian's gemstone depend on what month you're born in?"

"I guess it does. I never considered that, but it's possible."

"That must be the case!" By now, Saphir was pacing back and forth in thought. "And what if, depending on your gemstone, you had different powers? Or even different colors? Or—" He glanced at the ground. There was something written in the stone.

"What is this?" he said, crouching down to look at whatever was written. Saphir was shocked at what he read.

"Emer and Iridigrarr . . . friends to the end?" he read, now puzzled.

"What the—" Emer pushed him aside, touching the carved rock with her talon. She was staring at it with a mix of emotions on her face.

"Who's Iridigrarr?" Raider asked.

"He's no one." Emer backed away from the writing, wrapping her wings around her.

"Not from what I can tell," Saphir said. "It seems as if he was important."

"It's just that . . . agh, you know what? You don't need to worry about him." She waved her claws in frustration as smoke began to billow from her nose.

"If he makes you this upset—"

"DON'T WORRY ABOUT IRIDIGRARR!" Emer flared her wings and roared, fire storming out of her mouth. Saphir backed away in panic, shocked at his friend's behavior.

Emer folded her wings back, realizing what she had done. "Saphir . . . I'm sorry." She pressed her handlike claws to her forehead. "I shouldn't have acted that way."

Saphir cautiously approached her. "It's okay. You can tell me what's wrong."

Emer sighed. "Saphir . . . there's something I've been hiding from you and Paris and Gabby. Something important."

Saphir listened.

"Before I met you and Gabby and even Paris, I had another friend. We were very close, like siblings. That dragon I'm talking about is Iridigrarr, the name written on this stone."

"He must have been important to you," Saphir said.

Emer whished out a puff of smoke. "Not just to me," she said. "To the whole Bluescale tribe. Back then, I wasn't alone. I wasn't left out because of my differences. I had someone just like me as my friend."

"Are you saying that—"

"I'm saying that I wasn't the only dragon like myself. Iridigrarr was a Dralerian."

CHAPTER 13

IRIDIGRARR

Emer had just told Saphir her deepest secret.

He looked shocked.

"There was another Dralerian?" he questioned, amazement in his voice.

Emer nodded. "Yes. There's a long story about Iridigrarr, if you would like to hear it."

Saphir sat back on his haunches. "I want to hear it."

Emer gulped. It was time to tell Saphir the story about Iridigrarr. "Okay, I'll tell you." She took a deep breath and began.

"One night, during a violent snowstorm, Knifeclaw was doing a patrol over the land. Everything was normal, except for one difference."

"What was it?" Saphir asked.

"He found dragon eggs out in the snow. Knifeclaw took them back to the Bluescale cave, where Iridigrarr and I hatched a few months apart. When they saw we were not only Bluescales but Bluescales with gemstones, all the dragons were shocked. All Dralerian dragons were assumed to be extinct! After much debate, they came to a conclusion: Iridigrarr was to live at the Bluescale cave, and I was to live with the humans."

"Okay," Saphir said. "You and Iridigrarr were left out on the mountains in a snowstorm, and you turned out to be Dralerian Bluescales. But how did you transform into a human when you were an infant?"

"That I don't know," Emer said. "It happened such a long time ago. However, I do know they brought me to a city far from where any dangerous dragons or humans could find me. Knifeclaw brought me up to Fargo, North Dakota, and left me at a church. Someone obviously adopted me, because I live in a house with my mom."

"Wow. Interesting history," Saphir said.

"Iridigrarr was a Bluescale who stood out from the rest. Unlike the others, Iridigrarr had red scales and a garnet gemstone. He was kind, smart, and an awesome warrior with amazing elemental skills. Iridigrarr was my best friend."

"But what happened?" Saphir asked, caution and hesitation in his voice.

Emer sighed. She didn't want to say, but she had to. It was weighing down on her chest; she had to get it out. "It was my first battle," she told him. "Majesty and Knifeclaw decided to raid the Bloodclaws' cave to take back the Dark Energy Crystal. Majesty, Knifeclaw, and the other larger and stronger fighters would attack the front of the cave to distract the Bloodclaws, while Iridigrarr and I, who were smaller and nimble, would sneak through the passageways to their treasure room."

"That's how you knew how to enter the cave!" Raider exclaimed.

She nodded. "Taking the Dark Energy Crystal back was not an easy task. You can't handle the Dark Energy Crystal unless you are wearing special gloves, or else you turn evil. Iridigrarr handled the crystal and placed it into a bag by my side."

She knew what part was coming up in her story. She could see it clearly in her mind. "We began to exit the cave but were stopped. A Bloodclaw had managed to find us. He was wearing a device on his claw that was sharpened in the fashion of a knife. He cornered me. This beast, this awful beast, prepared to bring his weapon down on me to kill me."

"Why didn't you fight him?" Saphir asked.

"I froze out of fear. I had practiced fighting so many times, and I froze in battle because I got scared," Emer snarled.

"So, what happened?"

Emer saw the vivid, violent scene in her head, clearer than ever before. "Iridigrarr shoved me aside. He got stabbed instead."

Saphir's jaw dropped.

"The two began to fight. There was blood. Blood everywhere. I could only stand and watch, horrified." Emer felt tears began to trickle out of her eyes. "Iridigrarr managed to defeat the Bloodclaw . . . but . . ."

"But what?"

"Iridigrarr was fatally wounded," she said, voice shak-

ing. "I tried to tell him I would carry him back, but he argued with me. He told me to leave him there. To leave him behind. That it would be too much of a burden to carry him. That I might get killed too while trying to do so, and the Bluescales couldn't afford to lose both of us." Emer felt her wings shaking. "I had no other option. I had to leave him there for the good of all Bluescales."

Saphir drew in a quick, shocked breath.

"I told the others he had been killed while saving me. We managed to get the Dark Energy Crystal, but we lost an important dragon because of it. I was alone for a long time. I blamed myself for what happened. I blamed myself for leaving him there, for not standing up to the Bloodclaw. I yelled at myself, 'Why did I let Iridigrarr die?'"

That's when Emer, the strong, powerful Dralerian warrior, broke.

She collapsed on the ground, sobbing. She cried for every dragon she couldn't save from the Bloodclaws, for her lost friend Iridigrarr, for her hope that this war, this war that imprisoned all the good and kind dragons, would end.

She felt something drape over her.

Emer looked up. Saphir was standing above her, his wing draped over her quivering back.

"It's not your fault," he said. "None of this is."

She sniffed and then began to sit up.

"Don't worry." Saphir smiled at her, his green eyes glinting in the evening sunlight.

"Okay," she said, wiping the tears from her eyes and rustling her wings. "We should head back to the Bluescale cave. It won't be long before Knifeclaw is scouring the mountains looking for us."

"You're sure you're ready to head back? After what just happened?" Saphir asked, concerned.

"Y-yeah," she stuttered. "I can head back. I-I actually feel better than before."

"You do?"

Emer nodded. "Yes. I guess it's just good to get those things off my mind. If he were still here, I wouldn't be close friends with you or Gabby or Paris. You probably wouldn't be here next to me, either, and you wouldn't have your Dralerian form."

"In other words, you're okay?"

"Yes." She smiled at him.

Saphir grinned back. "Good."

And if any lost hikers had been watching, they would have seen two blue dragons take off into the sunset-filled sky.

CHAPTER 14

BLOODCLAW ATTACK

"So that's why you hate Bloodclaws so much," Saphir said. "They took your best friend away from you."

Emer nodded. "That's why I hate them, especially Demonheart. But I try to not think about them a lot."

Saphir flapped his wings in the evening sky. "Why?"

"If you think about something you hate too much, it goes from your brain to your heart and takes control of you." She landed on the Flight Ledge leading into the Bluescale cave, bouncing with grace onto the stone beneath her.

Saphir had watched her, and he did his best to hover the way she did. However, he lost his balance and fell to the stone ground with a mighty THUD.

"Ouch."

Emer helped him up with a smile on her face. "Tomorrow, I'll teach you how to land." The two dragons walked through the entryway into the long, dark hallway.

"That will definitely be fun," Saphir said, sarcasm lacing his words. "I can't wait to flop like a pancake onto the stone ground forty feet below me."

"Hey, it won't be that bad," Emer said, poking his arm. "I know you'll get the hang of it." She smiled at her friend.

Saphir smiled back, happiness glinting in his eyes. But it suddenly vanished as his scales stood on end and his wings shivered. "Why did it get so cold?" he chattered.

"Cold?" Emer asked, confused. "It's not cold in—" Shivers ran up her scales as what seemed like a blast of cold air hit her. It felt as if the very blood running through her veins was freezing. But Emer knew this was not a reaction to the air around them; the air was plenty warm. She knew dragons reacted to energy changes around them, whether good or bad.

This sudden chill meant there was something sinister nearby.

"Saphir," she said, "you need to keep an eye out for anything that looks like trouble."

"Why?" He shivered.

"You're not cold," Emer whispered to him.

"What?" Saphir asked in disbelief.

"There's something very bad near us."

CLICK-CLACK-CLICK-CLACK. The eerie echo of dragon claws resonated through the dark hallway.

Emer and Saphir stayed as still as the stone around them. The click-clack sound grew closer and closer.

Glowing yellow eyes flashed through the dim hallway. Slit pupils pierced through the dark to the two Dralerians.

A Bloodclaw.

"Saphir, stay behind me," Emer whispered. "I don't need you getting hurt. And if you think there's a chance I will die, shoot a burst of fire at the Bloodclaw. Okay?"

Saphir nodded.

Emer crept forward. The yellow eyes followed her every move.

"HEY!" a blast of green flame sprang from Bella's mouth, illuminating the hallway. "WHO ARE YOU?"

"Argree nar artook." The Bloodclaw's voice slithered in its bizarre language.

I wish they would speak normally, Emer grumbled to herself. *They're evil, and none of us can understand a word they say.* She glanced up.

The glowing eyes were gone.

Emer's heart pounded against her chest. "But . . . how . . . I saw it . . ." she said to herself, frightened. Her eyes scanned every inch of the dark hallway in a panicked frenzy, but to no avail.

"Is everything okay?" Saphir asked, concerned.

"Uh . . . yeah," she said hesitantly. Emer breathed in and out, regaining her confidence. "WHERE ARE YOU?" she demanded into the darkness, trying to summon the demon stalking her. Angry, she let a firestorm out of her mouth.

A Bloodclaw leaped through the flames, its teeth glinting in the emerald glow from her fire. A gleaming metal weapon on its front claw was raised above her. The Bloodclaw's eyes were glistening with evil, hatred, the pleasure of killing.

Screaming, Emer flapped backward, rolling sideways, hitting the side of the hallway with a SMASH.

Emer looked at her enemy, pain seething through her scales.

The Bloodclaw was ready to kill.

But not Emer, the Dralerian warrior.

Saphir.

Anger seized her body and threw her at the Bloodclaw. She roared in fury as she pinned the wicked beast onto the wall.

It screeched and swung its metal claw up in defense, slicing her face.

Emer thought a torn wing membrane hurt. This was a million times worse.

Ignoring the searing pain as best she could, her claws flashed emerald green and tore the skin on the claw that dealt her damage. Blood poured from the wound.

The Bloodclaw screeched in agony.

She dragged her other claw across the Bloodclaw's face. It screeched again.

Raising up her right talon, the emerald scales dull with blood, she smashed it down with all the strength in her body through the Bloodclaw's undefended chest.

It screamed a feeble screech and then crumpled into a bloody red heap.

Blood stained the walls and floor.

Emer heaved in breaths of air. Her fury was gone. The pain shooting through her face returned. She covered the injury with her bloodstained talon.

Saphir ran up to his friend. "Are you okay?"

"I guess." She lifted her talon from her face. Fresh blood droplets trickled down her now light-blue claws. Pain was crawling through her scales, and blood splatters covered the wall and floor nearby.

"Ugh, this is a mess!" Saphir muttered, eyeing the blood around him.

"Yeah, I assume you didn't think we would die." Emer glared at him.

"I tried breathing fire!" he exclaimed, defending himself. "I tried it! None came out!"

"Hmm," Emer said, looking at him. "That's weird. I'll have to look into that."

"HELP!" a familiar voice cried, its sound echoing down the hallway.

"Stonehorn!" Emer panicked, running toward the voice.

"Emer! What are you doing?" Saphir exclaimed, blocking her way. "You just got hurt!"

"I got hurt when trying to save you and the others from the Bloodclaws!" she growled. "Did that stop me?"

Saphir opened his mouth to argue but shut it again. "Okay," he said, "but I'm coming with you."

The two dragons dashed down the dark hall, following the distressed voice. As they ran along, the GlowCrystals returned, lighting the cave with their orange glow.

Emer and Saphir came to an opening in the hallway, from where the plea for help was coming. They entered the room and saw a horrific site: Stonehorn was lying on his side, a large gash underneath his wing. Blood seeped from the wound.

"Stonehorn!" Emer gasped, running up to him. "What happened?"

He wheezed in a breath, looking up at the two Dralerians. "I was teaching your human friends about the Bluescale cave when two Bloodclaws appeared out of nowhere! One of them began to fight with me. I've never fought, so he knocked me over. The other one snatched up the two children. The one with a metal claw was preparing to stab me when he heard a noise. Losing focus, he missed and sliced my side instead, knocking me out."

"That must have been us he heard!" Saphir exclaimed.

"Well, that nasty Bloodclaw is gone now. I defeated him." Emer lifted her bloodstained claws to show Stonehorn.

He winced in disgust. "That's an awful mess we'll have to clean up."

"The mess doesn't matter right now," Emer growled. "Helping you does."

"And finding the others," Saphir said in a determined voice. "I'll go and find them!" He dashed down another hallway before Emer could protest.

"Saphir!" she yelled, but to no avail. "Ugh, crazy non-listener," she grumbled to herself, glancing up at a tapestry.

Wait a second, she realized. She ran over to the tapestry and shredded it off the wall. Walking over to Stonehorn, she tied the ripped tapestry around his wound.

"That will have to do for now," she said, helping him stumble to his feet.

"Ah, thank you, Emer," Stonehorn said, standing again, shaking like a tree in the wind.

"We need to get you to Vladmir." She grimaced, helping him walk.

"HELP!" a voice screamed. A thunderous roar sounded, followed by an agonized screech.

"Saphir!" Emer yelled. She began to run forward, but then she stopped.

Stonehorn was with her.

How would she rescue both Stonehorn and her friends? She knew her friends would lose against the Bloodclaws, and they'd probably die. But Stonehorn, if he waited for too long, would be on the verge of dying himself.

"Emer," he said, interrupting her thoughts, "I see what you're doing. Go save your friends."

She looked at him. "But you're injured as well. I can't just drag you into a bloody battle where you have a chance of being killed."

"I'll be fine. Bring me with you."

"Are you sure?"

He nodded and then wobbled, losing his balance. Emer quickly ran over and supported him.

"Fine. But you have to stay back," she warned, beginning to walk forward with him.

It took much longer to find her friends than she had hoped. Too many images of her friends, dead and torn apart, flashed through her mind.

But at least I know that Stonehorn will be safe.

Fire blasted out of a nearby room, and screaming ensued.

That has to be the room! "Stonehorn, you'll be fine if I leave you right here?"

"Yes, I'm fine."

Emer helped him sit on the ground.

"Okay," she said warily, and then she charged into the room.

She stopped abruptly.

Her three friends were trying to fight off the other Bloodclaw. Saphir was defending Paris and Gabby, while Paris and Gabby were hurling rocks at the beast. Furious, the Bloodclaw lunged forward, hurling a fire-breath at Saphir. Saphir held up his arm in defense, wincing as the flame licked his scales a dull blue black. The beast flared his wings and swept Saphir aside, scratching the Bluescale's burned arm in the process. The Dralerian smashed into a wall and then crumpled to the ground, not dead or unconscious but very weak.

Paris hurled more rocks at the Bloodclaw, only to have it roar in a fury, lunge at her, and sweep her up in its crusty, bloodstained talons.

Gabby, seeing Paris was in danger, picked up the largest rock she could lift and hurled it at the monster.

CRACK!

It hit the Bloodclaw in the head, snapping its awful teeth, denting its jaw, and breaking its right devil horn.

"ARGREEAAAAAAAAAAR!" it screamed, making the stalactites above it shake. It slammed Paris to the ground and stormed forward. Smoke and even sparks poured out of its nostrils.

What the heck am I doing just standing here? a stunned Emer realized. *I have to go and help my friends!* She leaped into the air, spreading her wings into a small glide, and rammed her horns straight into the side of the rampaging Bloodclaw. Its ribs splintered with mighty SNAPS, and Emer sent the beast crashing into the wall.

SMASH! The beast hit the wall, and its left devil horn snapped off its head. It crumpled to the ground.

But of course it's not dead. The everlasting monster wobbled to its feet, shaking. It hissed, blasting fire at Emer. She rolled out of the way and then swept forward, clawing it in the stomach. Blood dripped out of the new cut.

Emer grabbed the Bloodclaw's last remaining horn and slammed its head into the wall with a CRACK. The Bloodclaw screeched, grappling at Emer's scales to create one wound, but it soon fell silent. Its body went limp.

And at that moment, though lots of damage had been done, Emer knew that she, her friends, and the whole Bluescale tribe were safe from danger—for now.

CHAPTER 15

PEACE AFTER THE FIGHT

A burst of flame shot into the room, followed by the elegant blue scales of Majesty, striding in hurriedly with great confidence. Vladmir's diamond-white scales and concerned face followed, and Knifeclaw's scarred scales followed close behind.

Emer couldn't have been happier that they'd shown up. Dashing over to them, she asked, "How did you find out about this?"

"Stonehorn telecommunicated me," Majesty said.

"Why didn't you do that, Emer?" Knifeclaw demanded. "Oh, wait. You must have been busy using your HUMAN SIDE again."

Smoke whished out of Emer's nose as angry thoughts rumbled through her mind.

"There is no time to argue now!" Vladmir huffed, hurling fabric bandages and herbal salve at the other dragons.

"We have to go and help the others, whether they're human or not!"

"You're right," Majesty agreed. "Emer, you go take care of your Dralerian friend. The rest of us will help the humans."

"Yes, sir," everyone said simultaneously. Emer rushed over to Saphir, who was trying to stand up. As soon as he put weight on his injured leg, he collapsed to the ground.

"You're hurt!" she exclaimed.

He tried to stand up again, but to no avail. So he propped himself up in an awkward sitting pose. "Oh, I'm fine, as good as ever," Saphir said, doing his best at sounding casual and brave.

Emer snickered at his attempt but knew he wasn't okay. "I saw you smash into the wall and get cut and get burned. You're not okay."

"How do you know I'm in pain?"

"You're holding your injured arm."

Saphir looked down. He had unconsciously been grasping the burned and cut arm. "Well," he stuttered, "I was just—"

"Let me help you," Emer said, reaching for the arm.

He yanked it away from her reach.

"I won't hurt you. I promise."

"Emer—"

"You'll be fine." She looked at him with kind eyes and eased his injured arm out of his defensive grasp.

With the greatest ease, she scooped up some of the herbal salve out of the stone jar; the mint-green slime stuck to her claws. Emer placed it onto the large gash.

"AAAAGH!" Saphir exclaimed, yanking his arm out of her grasp and trying to brush the slime off. To his dismay, the more he tried to brush the salve off, the more it stuck to his cut and burned scales.

"What's wrong?"

"The stuff stings! It STINGS!"

Emer sighed and then snatched his arm back into her grasp. Saphir tried to squirm away, but Emer held his arm firmly.

"It probably does sting," she said. "There's some herb in there that cleanses wounds. What herb that is, I don't know. I never got into the study of herbs anyway."

"Emer! Stop babbling and help me!" Saphir hissed.

Emer snapped back to focus. "The only way it will feel better is if I put more salve onto the wound," she said, scooping up more of the slimy concoction.

"Emer, why?"

"Because I know it will make you feel better!" she exclaimed. "When I look at the condition of your arm, I wince. I wouldn't be surprised if it scars! That's why I'm putting this salve onto it! I'm sorry if it hurts. I'm only trying to help you!"

He was silent. "Okay." His arm relaxed, and Emer was able to help him.

Emer lost herself in her surroundings for a while. She heard Majesty and Knifeclaw in debate; she heard Vladmir helping Paris from her terrible incident; and she heard Gabby comforting Paris, wondering why Emer wasn't there with them.

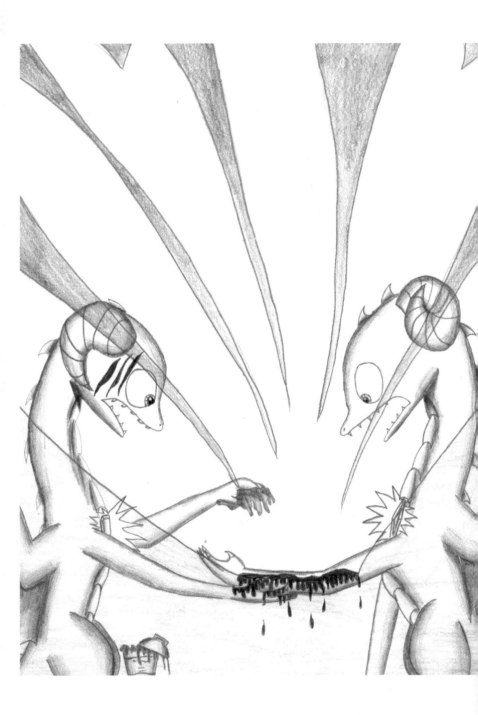

"Emer!" Saphir said, cutting off her train of thought.

"What?"

"Your emerald! It's glowing!"

"What?" she said, shocked. Looking down at her chest, she saw the green emerald was emitting a bright green light.

"What?" she muttered, confused. Glancing up, she realized Saphir's sapphire was releasing a blue light. "Saphir! Your sapphire!"

He glanced down, his eyes nearly bulging out in surprise. He opened his mouth to speak, but no words came out.

They glanced at Saphir's cut.

It looked as if something was glowing inside of it.

Emer peered at the cut but fell back as a bright white light streamed from the wound. Emer shut her eyes. Even after she did, she still saw white.

In a moment, it was gone. She opened her eyes, and blurry spots danced everywhere. When she rubbed her eyes, they went away. What she saw made her jaw drop.

Saphir's arm was as good as new. There was no scratch, no scar, no speck of dirt.

"Wow!" Emer gasped in amazement.

"I know," Saphir murmured, stroking one of his talons over the area where his cut had been. "The cut the Bloodclaw gave you earlier is gone, too."

"Seriously?"

"Yes."

Emer touched her face where the Bloodclaw had scratched her. Instead of feeling a bumpy, rough scab, she felt the smooth precision of her scales. "How did this happen?" she asked, astounded. Her mind could not even begin to grasp this concept. Did she have healing powers?

"I think our gemstones have something to do with it," Saphir mused. "They were glowing, after all."

"That's possible."

"Young Dralerians and humans!" a noble voice rang. Emer looked up. Majesty was talking. "Because of the threat of two Bloodclaws having somehow gotten past our guards, you will all spend the night in the Meeting Room guarded by Knifeclaw, Vladmir, and me! Prepare!"

* * * * *

The rest of the evening was a blur. Emer helped set up the Meeting Room for herself and her friends, and then they ate a delicious dinner of buffalo ribs. After supper, Knifeclaw pulled her aside to discuss the "pride of being a dragon." Then she talked with her friends some, but she was mostly silent in thought. At last, the crystals were put out, and everyone went to sleep.

Well, everyone except her.

Her mind was a racing blur of Bloodclaws, blood, fighting, and Knifeclaw growling, "Be a better dragon. Use your dragon side. Your human side is useless. Look at how well your friends did in fighting! They were terrible! Stick with us dragons; we will never fail you."

But my friends have never failed me, she whimpered in her mind. *My friends have always been there for me, no matter what. Even after I revealed my greatest secret to them, they still had faith in me.* She pulled the fur cover tightly around her. *I wish I knew what to do.*

"Emer."

"Who is it?" she whispered, her voice still sad from her thoughts.

"It's me, Saphir."

Emer sat up in a hurry. "Saphir!" she exclaimed in a loud whisper. "I thought you were asleep!"

"No, not yet," he said in a quiet tone back to her. "I sensed something. It wasn't like earlier today when we sensed that awful Bloodclaw, but my scales were tingling. I followed the feeling over to you. I guess you're upset."

Emer's jaw almost dropped. *How did he know?* the voice in her head screamed. "Uh, you probably just sensed something weird. I mean, I'm not upset at all! No, not upset," she babbled, worry in her voice.

Emer could make out Saphir giving her a look in the darkness. "You are such a bad liar," he said, laughing a little. "Honestly, what's wrong?"

She sighed, puffing a small plume of green fire; it illuminated the area around them. "I'm just worried about everything that happened earlier this evening. Bloodclaws haven't gotten into our cave for more than four hundred years. And, to be honest, I'm a little scared at what's happening," she whispered.

Saphir nodded. "Is that all?"

Her head wanted to say yes, but her heart screamed no. "No," she whispered, drifting her gaze from him to the floor.

"What is it?"

"Knifeclaw is against me being friends with you, Paris, and Gabby. He wants me to abandon you. He says that humans aren't as great as dragons and that you are terrible at battle, whereas dragons are much more reliable in battle. He wants me to use my dragon side more . . ." She trailed off, looking away from him.

"But you're not a dragon," Saphir said. "You're a Dralerian."

"So? Knifeclaw doesn't care." She flung her wings out in aggravation.

"Why can't you be both?" he asked. "Why can't you be both human and dragon, not just one or the other? There's a logical reason you have this ability, Emer, and I think you're meant to invest in both sides of who you are, not just strengthen one and abandon the other."

Emer looked at him, startled. *Is that what Vladmir has been trying to tell me to do for the past thirteen years?* she wondered. "Well . . . Saphir . . . I never really . . . um . . . considered that option . . ." she murmured. The more she thought about it, the more it seemed like a reasonable idea.

"And about the Bloodclaws invading the cave," he whispered.

"Yeah?"

"I don't think you have too much to worry about. I know they're murderous beasts from Hades, but you know how to handle them and keep your friends and the other Bluescales safe."

"But what if I fail?" she fretted. "What if I fail and lose

you and the others to the Bloodclaws? I don't want that to happen! You guys are my friends, and I never want to lose you like I lost Iridigrarr!" she cried, admitting her fear.

Emer tilted her head away from him, ashamed. Knifeclaw would yell at her for admitting her fear! Dragons were supposed to be the most fearsome beasts, afraid of nothing.

She felt something brush her wing. Emer looked up, only to realize Saphir's wing had brushed against hers.

"I don't think you'll let that happen," he whispered, more quietly than before.

"Why?"

"Because you care about us a lot, and I know you're the greatest warrior in this whole cave," he murmured.

Emer felt her face grow hot and a smile crawl along her mouth. "Geez," she laughed. "What happened to the shy boy I met at the start of the year?" She punched him in a playful way.

He shrugged and drew his wing back. "I guess he gained the power of a Dralerian," he said.

There was both an awkward and comforting silence between them.

"Good night, Emer," he whispered, tiptoeing away.

"Good night, Saphir," she whispered, the stupid smile still plastered onto her face as she snuggled back into her furs, falling into a peaceful, restful slumber.

* * * * *

Emer's eyes opened. The early morning light shone in through the light hole she often used as an entrance and exit.

Ack, what a night, she grumbled to herself, sitting up. In her dreams, Bloodclaws dripping with blood and burns had lunged at her, screaming, "Let us kill you! Let us hurt you! Let us drag our claws across your scales!" And Knifeclaw had stood by, ignoring her in the ruckus, growling, "You betrayer of dragonkind. You're not fit to be with us."

She shuddered at the mere recall of the dream. *At least that was only a silly little figment of my imagination and not reality,* she thought in relief. Glancing around, she remembered it was Saturday, probably about five in the morning.

Back to sleep. She lay back down on her bed to sleep for the few hours of rest she had remaining to her.

Something snagged her tail.

WHOOSH! She was dragged out from under her covers across the cool stone floor. Emer grappled the slick ground, trying to find a niche in the stone to keep her grasp.

"Help! HELP!" she screamed.

This only caused her to be yanked up from the floor to the wall faster. The chain, hooked firmly around her tail, dragged her through the light hole.

Emer turned around to breathe an angry storm of flames onto whomever did this, only to feel something hard smash down onto her head. CLONK!

Everything went black.

CHAPTER 16

DEMONHEART'S TORTURE

Ugh . . .

Emer's mind began to work again. She opened her bleary eyes just a crack. *Ow.* It hurt to open her eyes. In fact, her whole head hurt.

Whoa. Where am I? She glanced around. Even though everything was dark, Emer could make out some stone formations, a couple of stalactites, and . . . someone . . . something on the other side of the room.

"Hello?" she asked. Her voice bounced around the room. Standing up, she realized this room was warmer than the Bluescale cave, almost hot.

The thing laughed in the distance.

"Who are you?" she yelled with confidence, marching forward. *CLANK.* She couldn't move far. Glancing down, she realized there was a smooth black chain around her leg, pinning her to a wall nearby.

Torches flickered on in formation, illuminating the brown stone room around her. As she looked around, everything came together. She had been here before!

Emer looked straight ahead. Sitting before her, on a mighty throne carved from many precious stones, sat the one who was the cause of all her troubles: the overly large, blood-colored, evil-loving Demonheart, the leader of the Bloodclaws.

His evil eyes gleamed when he saw her. "Ah, my victim is awake," he said in a slithery tone, teeth and claws glinting in the torchlight.

"Demonheart," she growled, anger flooding her body. "What are you doing? Why am I here?" Smoke poured out of her nose.

"Tsk-tsk. Can't I just have a Bluescale over for tea?" he asked with innocence.

Emer glared at him. "If you gave any dragon tea, it would be laced with poison, you evil, heartless monster!" she yelled. "Get me out of this chain and let me leave, before I rip your throat out of your body and feed it to your sick followers!"

"Why, thank you for the compliment." He smiled at her, his expression filled with scorn. "Now that you are here, perhaps you will answer a few questions for me," he said, spreading his fearsome black wings to their full size.

"What questions?"

"Oh, I just want some random tidbits about The Foretelling and whether your puny human friends were part of it," he said casually. "Then I want to find them and convince them to be part of my colony instead of those prissy blue dragons' so-called colony."

"And what if they said no?" Emer hissed. "What if they told you to leave them alone?

"Oh, they would join me."

"Pfff," she scoffed at him.

"Because, if not, I would kill them."

Emer was silent.

"I'd probably kill them, anyway, after I was done using them," he mused. "Oh, how fun it would be to kill a human! I haven't done it for four hundred years!" He laughed with irritating glee and then focused his yellow eyes on Emer again. "And I will kill you, too, Emer! Oh, how fun this will be!"

"You will never put one of your crummy claws onto me or my friends," she growled, the smoke around her growing heavier.

"Why?" he asked. "I'm surprised you're not agreeing with me on this."

"What?"

"Oh, I thought you might be unhappy with your life. You know, because you're a Dralerian, you have no true dragon or human part to you. You're probably depressed and sad that no one will accept you. You are a cursed mistake, after all. Might as well wave bye-bye to your fake friends and that mother you have."

Emer stared at him, anger, shock, sadness, and fear jumping about in her mind. "How do you know about my power?"

"Look at you," he continued, ignoring her. "Your dragon side is honored by many dragons but frightening and even demon-like to humans. Your human side is useful to your human colony but demoralizing and weak to the dragons. You're nothing but a cursed mistake that was made by the Greatwing."

"That's . . . that's not true!"

"One day, your human society will find out and shun you from their life and then go and kill off all your dragon friends. Your remaining dragon friends will abandon you, blaming you for the cause of their troubles, which will be correct for them to do. Then you will have no one, no one at all in your life."

"I have friends!" Emer screamed in response to his taunting. "I have my mother! I have my friends, Gabby, Paris, and Saphir! All the Bluescales in the cave have faith in me, even Knifeclaw!" She clawed forward despite her restraint, which seemed to be pulling apart from her yearning to end this corrupt beast in front of her, weaving lies into her mind.

"You will never get anywhere in this world. Why hope?"

CRACK!

"Because you always need something to look forward to!"

CRACK!

"Why even hope!" Demonheart yelled, becoming angry. "There is no hope!"

CRACK!

"Because hope is what keeps you fighting against everything evil in the world!" she yelled, thoughts flowing through her mind. "You take so much from us other dragons!" she screamed. "You took away our independence! Our freedom! My friend! You deserve to die!"

CRACK!

"And yet, you have killed so many of my loyal follow- ers," he growled, smoke beginning to stream out of his nose. "Doesn't that make you as evil as I?"

SNAP! The chain broke, and Emer tore free from the stone beneath her to fly up at this evil dragon. She released an explosion of green fire, hoping to obliterate him.

But something blocked it.

Scareye.

The two dragons slammed to the ground, angry as ever. Emer glanced up at Demonheart and realized he was grasping his neck. *Good, I burned him some.*

She looked at Scareye in front of her. Most of his scales were now a charred black. Scareye was panting, his black tongue hanging limply from between his teeth. "You . . . you almost killed Demonheart," he growled, slit eyes bulg- ing out at this concept.

"Indeed I did," she growled back, feeling almost a pity for this dragon she would soon kill. He looked weak from the fire attack she had hit him with.

Scareye shrieked, low at first and then rising to an ear- splitting volume. "DIE!" he screamed, lunging forward, ob- sidian-black claws hungry for blood.

Emer dodged his attack and raked her claw down his wing.

"AAAGH!"

"That is my revenge for doing that to me!" she hissed, recalling the same pain he had given to her. Grabbing his other wing, she tore her claw down it, ripping away some

scaly skin. Blood dripped down her talons as the dragon reared up and attacked her, pulling his claws along her scales. Pain seared through her whole body.

Flaring her wings with anger, Emer sent Scareye slamming to the floor beneath her. Bringing forth an emerald claw, she slammed it down at his chest, feeling it plunge into his bloody flesh.

Fire stormed out of Scareye's mouth as he convulsed from the pain. Then he fell limp as his eyes shut forever, the remaining smoke trickling out of his nostrils.

Drawing her claw out of his chest cavity, she glared up to meet Demonheart's yellow eyes.

But there were none.

Demonheart, the heartless monster, had disappeared.

Grumbling under her breath, she began to calculate a way out of the cave.

A small stone plopped onto her head.

Oh no! The cave is collapsing! She panicked, moving out of the way as dirt and stone toppled to the ground where she once stood.

"Is there anyone down there?" a voice said softly.

"Paris?" Emer asked, walking toward the small pile of debris.

"Emer!" Paris exclaimed, leaning over the hole she had made. "You're okay! Covered with blood and scratches, but okay!"

"How did you guys find me?"

"I heard cries of help earlier this morning," Gabby explained. "I woke up and saw you were gone. I alerted the others. Saphir and Knifeclaw figured the Bloodclaws had kidnapped you for interrogation, so—"

"Gabby and I rode on Saphir's back out of the Blues-cale cave, and Knifeclaw led the way to where he thought you would be!" Paris exclaimed, interrupting Gabby. "Our plan was to enter through this hole, save you, and burn the whole place down!"

"Actually," Saphir corrected, "our plan was to dig the hole, find you, and save you from the Bloodclaws."

"I already saved myself! Scareye is dead, and Demon-heart is wounded!"

"Seriously?" Paris as well as Gabby, Saphir, and Knife-claw exclaimed.

"Yes!" She flew into the hole they had made, greeting the astounded faces of her friends and Knifeclaw.

"You . . . you killed Scareye?" Knifeclaw said with amazement. "And—and injured Demonheart? How?"

"By using my human smarts and my dragon strength," Emer responded with confidence. "I'll explain everything that happened on the way back home."

CHAPTER 17

THE GEMSTONE WARRIORS

One and a half weeks later . . .

"Bella! Come on!" Paris yelled into Bella's ear.

"Ugh," Bella grumbled, rubbing her ear. "This is coming from the girl who wanted to stay at the Bluescale cave for the rest of her life."

Paris sighed and pulled Bella away from her locker. "Let's go!" she said, dashing down the hallway

"Okay, I'm coming!" Bella yelled, running up to Paris. *Ah, how great it is to not have to worry!* Bella thought, a smile on her face. *My friends know who I am: a Dralerian. And I know that I don't have to abandon my human side for my dragon side, as Knifeclaw says. I can use both to my advantage!*

"So everyone else here has no recollection of what happened last Thursday?" Paris asked, looking amazed and confused at the same time.

"Vladmir said a strange wave of energy erased the memory of the attack from anyone who had seen or heard of the attack except for us," Bella said, running alongside her friend.

"I still don't get it," Paris grumbled, shaking her head as she dashed into the library. "How does he know it took away the memory from the other humans?"

"I don't know," Bella said, plunking down into a chair where Gabby and Raider were sitting. "Well? Are we on time?"

"Hmmm," Raider considered, looking at his watch. "You're late by one second!"

"But otherwise, I was on time?"

"I told you! You were late by one second!"

"Raider!" Gabby huffed. "Cut it out!"

"Yeah," Paris said, "we have to get focused on our work. What topic did you want us to do today?" she asked Bella, dumping her backpack of books onto the table and skimming through them. "Science? Math? Language?"

"Music?" Gabby asked.

"Computers?" Raider asked.

Glancing around, Bella made sure no one else was in the library. "Dragons!" she exclaimed.

"Dragons?" Paris asked, confused. She picked up her books and skimmed through them, the pages flying. Slamming her book down, she said, "There's no topic about dragons in our studies."

"Not our studies," Bella grinned. "In life! With the Bluescales!"

"Oh," Paris said. "That makes more sense. But why did you call this a school meeting?"

"Oh, hush, Paris," Gabby scoffed. "What do you want to say, Bella?"

"Okay," she said, excitement gleaming in her eyes, "you know how we all fought against the Bloodclaws and lived?"

"Yes, barely," the other three said in unison.

She gave a pretend glare at her friends. "Yes, that is true. But what if we four created an elite team to fight against the Bloodclaws and help not just the Bluescales but all of dragonkind?"

"That sounds like a lot of work," Gabby said.

"Work? This team idea sounds fun!" Paris exclaimed. "We can pummel those red worms' stupid butts!" She leaped upon the table, striking a brave pose.

Bella couldn't help but laugh at this.

"Would you help me with my fighting skills?" Raider asked. "I'm a lousy fighter."

"I'm not the best, either," Gabby agreed.

"I'm an awesome fighter!" Paris grinned. "Smash! Ka-pow!" she punched the air and jumped about on the table, books sliding off in her excitement.

"I wouldn't say any of us are bad fighters," Bella disagreed.

"What?" her friends asked in disbelief.

"All of you did your best," she said. "Raider, you defended Paris and Gabby from the Bloodclaw that infiltrated the cave. Paris, you stood up against all those beasts, hurling anything you could find at them."

"Aw, no need to thank me." Paris grinned with sass. "I hurl rocks at evil, soulless dragons all the time!"

"And, Gabby—"

"NO! I know I failed!" Gabby cried, covering her face.

"No! You stood up to the Bloodclaw when it was threatening Paris. You hurled a humongous rock at it and knocked one of its horns off."

"Really?" Gabby asked, surprised.

"Yes!"

"I probably dealt the most damage to myself," Raider said. "I'm surprised I'm not a pancake right now!"

"Yeah, you were pretty terrible at landing when I saw you," Paris mused.

Raider glared at her.

"We'll improve those landing skills," Bella reassured him. "And your fighting skills. And find your dragon fire."

"Wait," Gabby said. "What will our parents say about this? If they knew we kept going to this hidden cave full of dragons, they'd ground us for life and demolish the dragons!"

"I'd be in the most trouble," Raider said. "I just became a Dralerian!"

"We'll keep it a secret," Bella said. "We'll just tell them we formed a club and that our clubhouse is out in West Fargo."

"And what about Demonheart?" Gabby asked, now worried. "What if he decides to attack our school and the Bluescales again? Is it even safe to be here?"

"We'll punch him in the face if he dares set foot near us!" Paris yelled, punching a bookshelf nearby.

"I injured Demonheart, and from what I can gather, he won't set foot outside his throne room until he's well again," Bella said. "Besides, it was very risky sending out all those dragons in front of humans. I don't understand why he did it."

"That's good." Gabby sighed with relief.

"Anyway," Paris said. "What should we call our team? I was thinking of Paris's Pummelers!" She spread her hands out with drama.

"No!" Raider scoffed, rolling his eyes. "Raider's Raptors sounds much more fearsome!"

"Both your ideas are lame!" Gabby said. "Gabby's Grinders is by far the most fearsome!"

"No! Mine is best!"

"No! Mine!"

"No!"

"Uh, guys?" Bella asked, interrupting her friends' squabble.

"Yes?" they all asked.

"How about the Gemstone Warriors?" she suggested. "Because two of the members are Dralerians, and no one's name is at the beginning."

"Hmm." They all thought about it.

"I think it's a good name," Raider said.

"It's cool!" Gabby agreed.

"I like it!" Paris said. "It's not as cool as Paris's Pummelers, but the Gemstone Warriors has a nice ring."

"It's settled!" Bella said, ecstatic.

"We are the Gemstone Warriors," Paris said, adventure in her voice. "We help all who are good and kick the bad dragons' sorry butts!"

"And with two Dralerians, humans who can transform to dragons, on the team, using both their dragon and human side to help the good," Raider added, looking at Bella.

"As well as the human warriors!" Gabby grinned, punching the air.

"I can say one thing for sure," Bella said. "Bloodclaws, look out. We're ready to fight!"

CHAPTER 18

A HIDDEN HELPER

A dragon sat, waiting.

He was waiting for someone important to come to him.

Or, rather, my superior boss who always tells me what to do, he growled in his head. *Arrogant beast, always wanting to prove himself right and killing anyone and everyone in his way.*

His gem-encrusted door creaked open.

A Bloodclaw stepped into the room. The waiting dragon immediately knew it was Demonheart. Demonheart's large size and black markings on his eyes said it all. There was a white bandage on his neck with yellow liquid oozing out.

Demonheart did not look happy. In fact, he looked furious as he approached the special dragon.

"So, I take it you carried out the plan I suggested," the dragon on the throne said carefully.

"Yeeeeeesss." Demonheart made the word slither. "And like all your other plans, it FAILED!" Fire whirled out of his mouth in an angry storm, making black marks on the brown stones around him.

"What happened?"

"Oh, we bombarded the school just as you said and found The Chosen Ones there, just as you said. But then, those dratted Bluescales attacked, with Emer the Bluescale warrior there, attacking us with all her fury!"

"You mean the Dralerian Warrior. Honestly, how many times do I have to tell you?"

"It doesn't matter!" Demonheart roared, shaking the cave. "She managed to sneak into our cave and steal the humans, making them side with the Bluescales!" He slashed his black talons across a stalagmite, a large gash forming in the stone.

"But I suggested two other plans to get The Chosen Ones back, as well as capture Emer," the golden-taloned dragon said, flicking a speck of stone off his bright red scales.

"She killed the dragons we sent to infiltrate their cave!" Demonheart stormed as smoke from his nose filled the room. "Then when we kidnapped her, she injured me and killed Scareye!"

"Finally, she killed someone who needed to go."

Demonheart lunged forward, yanking the golden-yellow ram horns on the other dragon's head. "Scareye was quite useful to all of us," Demonheart growled, too close for comfort. "Now with him gone, you'll have to take his place and activate your power." He jabbed the dragon's chest. Demonheart's claw slid across the golden chest plates.

"Oh, I'll help you," the bright red dragon agreed. "But there's one problem."

"What?"

"My power is weak. I've never used it."

Demonheart growled, "What do you need?"

"The Dark Energy Crystal."

Demonheart paused and then said, "You're insane. We've lost enough Bloodclaws already. We can't afford to send anyone else back into that cold Bluescale cave."

"Yes, but what is the loss of a few Bloodclaws if they scare the Bluescale cave into even more anger and fear? And what is the loss of a few Bloodclaws for the future of the world?"

"Hmm . . ." Demonheart considered. "What is the loss of a few Bloodclaws if it will help us gain our fair revenge on the dragons—and the extinction of the humans?"

"As well as the death of Emer." The other dragon grinned, revealing his sinister smile. "Once I have the Dark Energy Crystal, we can end Emer, end The Chosen Ones, end the humans, and put all other dragons, including the Bluescales, into slavery."

"I can't believe I'm even asking you this," Demonheart growled. "But what is your plan to bring the Dark Energy Crystal back into our talons?"

"Simple." The golden-horned dragon snickered. "Send two Bloodclaws to the cave at night in disguise. Have them take the Dark Energy Crystal and kill anyone who might have seen them. When Emer finds out, she'll come here to fight us. But I'll trap her and rip that precious emerald of hers right out of her chest."

"Good plan for a dragon a rank below me," Demon-heart growled. "I'll think about it." He prowled out of the room, slamming the door behind him.

But I know he'll do it, the bright red dragon thought in his cunning mind. With his golden-yellow talons, he felt the scar on his side carefully and then tapped the red garnet gemstone on his chest.

"Or else my name isn't Iridigrarr."

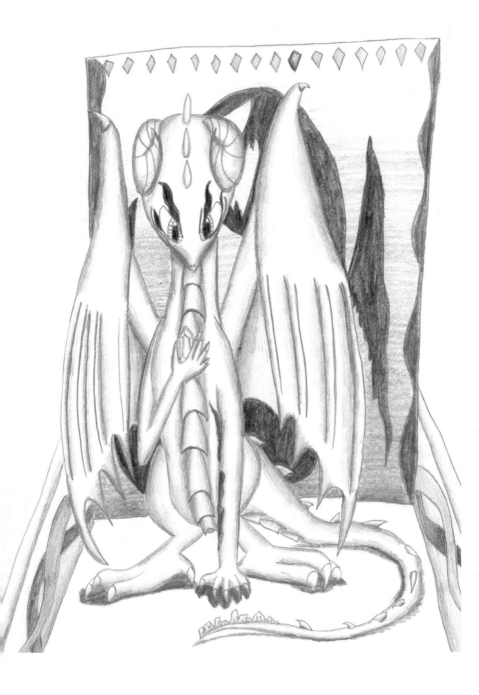

ACKNOWLEDGEMENTS

To Mom, for everything. For inspiring me to never give up, to follow my dreams, and to try new things. For motivating me turn my story into a book. For helping me when I had writer's block. For always being positive and believing in me. For teaching me to work hard for what I want and believe that anything is possible.

To Grandma LaValle, my writing coach, for helping me with the very first edits of my book before we even went to the publishers, laughing over the funny tidbits in the story, and teaching me crucial knowledge about writing, grammar, and the English language.

To Papa for helping with my book and putting up with my story that consumed the women in his life.

To my art teacher, Emily Williams-Wheeler, for having faith in my illustrations and encouraging me that I could do it, teaching me important art techniques and skills, and helping me develop my artistic abilities.

To Beaver's Pond Press, which includes:

Lily, for having faith in my story and taking it into the family of books and authors there.

Hanna, the project manager, for giving me guidance, help, and support along this amazing journey.

Lisa, the developmental editor, for giving me advice on writing I had never heard before and for helping me make my story shine brighter than it had before.

Laura, the copyeditor, for finding all the little things that hid from me that had to be tweaked and for teaching me new facts about writing.

Dan, the designer, for laying out my book, creating an awesome cover, and helping to fix any minor edits.

And to all the people out there who have encouraged me to write, listened to my work, and have big, bright, wonderful imaginations that shine brighter than the stars.

ABOUT THE AUTHOR

Izzyanna Andersen is a fifteen-year-old with a love of dragons. She's been passionate about books and art as long as she can remember, and has been drawing and writing small stories and poems from an early age. Izzy began to write and illustrate The Power of the Gemstones: Revealing her Secret when she was thirteen.

When she is not writing or drawing, she can be found singing, dancing, playing piano, going to the lake, or hanging out with her friends. She currently resides in Minnesota with her mom, two brothers, two dogs, two parrots, and a closet full of dragons.

For more information, visit www.thepowerofthegemstones. com or follow Izzyanna Andersen and The Power of the Gemstones on Facebook.

Be prepared for what's to come in Book 2...!